RHODES

THE CARETAKERS

Also by M.M. Gornell

Rhodes – The Movie-Maker
Rhodes — The Mojave-Stone
Counsel of Ravens
Reticence of Ravens
Lies of Convenience
Death of a Perfect Man
Uncle Si's Secret

RHODES

THE CARETAKERS

M. M. Gornell

Champlain Avenue Books, Inc.
Las Vegas, Nevada

International Standard Book Number ISBN- 978-1-943063-48-2

Library of Congress LCN: 2019942842

FIRST EDITION
2019

Printed in the United States of America

To:

Virginia "Dinna" Moody

PREFACE

For the few among many who have ventured this way and settled down—the Mojave Desert provides a unique and sometimes revealing perspective for their lives. Indeed for some, Route 66 itself becomes a directional beacon toward their place in our world. For a *selected few* of these *selected few*, it can also become a much-needed *place* of respite.

A sanctuary. A place where hitherto held perceptions are allowed to shift, sometimes even double-back on themselves. No longer needed "pasts" are blown away—riding in the rush of a dust-laden Mojave wind gust. *Dispatched to who-knows-where.*

Part One

Let the Game Begin

PROLOGUE

A few years back, Lucien "Lucca" Fabero planted a Brown Turkey fig, a Chicago Hardy fig, and a Bartlett pear tree directly in line of sight out his kitchen window.

Now, both figs were producing very nicely. But disappointingly so far, his pear tree would become full with beautiful white flowers in spring, but little fruit by fall. Only two steadfast pale green pears survived this last Mojave summer. Fortunately, desert gardening was his cherished challenge and Lucca figured he was doing pretty well at it on most fronts. *Except for my pears.*

He even wanted to try growing more edibles—grapes were next on his list, and Lucca smiled at the thought of his cuttings sitting in a glass vase of water on the eastern-facing windowsill in his spare bedroom. "How lucky I am." *Being able to do what I like doing. And having a place to do it in.*

This Sunday morning, he took the time to have a second cup of black coffee and further enjoy "smelling" the morning while appreciating his life from his warm comfy kitchen. Through his window, he could additionally see wind-swirling dust devils rushing down the piece of Shiné Road visible through the Athol trees lining the property. Closer in, his little orchard-patch was unaffected. Calm. The wind tunnels around them were unique and he had planted his trees appropriately.

Lucca continued smiling.

His father lived to be one-hundred and three years old. His father's father, however, only made it to ninety-nine. Both proclaimed whenever asked, "A Lucky Strike and a finger of Anisette every morning" were the keys to their good health. A self-serving comment, Lucca thought. Nevertheless, their genes were his genes—and being neither a smoker nor drinker himself, Lucca expected to spend many more years as the Rhodes caretaker.

His smile remained, but now he also sighed.

These days, his only company was his daughter, Jasmine. *The heartbeat of my life.* He had no sons, but Lucca didn't really care about passing on a family name. Jasmine was more than any father could ask for. Beautiful, loving, dutiful—and oh-so-smart. *Except when it came to that idiot she married.*

"Oh well," Lucca said aloud. Work beckoned. He had let the gasoline in his truck get below a quarter, and he wanted a full tank before going into Barstow for supplies. "Better top up from one of the spare cans in the shed." He maintained several five-gallon gasoline containers just for occasions like this.

Chapter One

Match Arranged, Board Setup, Opponents in Place, and Timer Primed

From LC's journal: Darned Desert. Sometimes it does get to me. When the wind's a blowing like this, it's hell. Used to curse more, heavy-duty sometimes, but Viola's fussed me out so much about it, can't hardly even write a swear word no more. Damn, do I love that woman.

Saturday Morning: Somewhere on California I-40 between Newberry Springs and Barstow, CA

"Darned desert," Ben whispered to himself. Since his words were for his ears only, he allowed a petulant overlay of distaste to color his tone.

So much difference a day can make.

Yesterday morning—while the Caltrans workers lowered the massive culvert section into place—California Highway Patrol Officer Benjamin Bellaeu fancied the cranes themselves were grunting and groaning as the massive concrete-encased culvert swayed and bounced with the wind before finally coming to rest in its new home destination. *And rather gracefully*, Ben had further mused. *If such a word as graceful could be applied to a*

1

construction-type task such as culvert-lowering. And perfect. Artful even. Especially *given* the size of the huge concrete encased tunnel piece, and *given* desert winds were gusting fierce enough through the work area to create a dustbowl-hell.

Both days he also witnessed breath-pausing sunrises. Thus, with perverse insistence this Saturday morning, Ben willfully continued to ignore Caltrans-congratulatory thoughts, and striated deep red-to-pastel horizons, and encouraged his emotions and thoughts to wallow in the negative aspects of his current situation.

Last night is what makes the difference.

On his arrival this morning—now feeling like hours ago— he had positioned the driver's seat of his parked Black-and-White as far back as it would go to maximize his front area. Consequently, he was now thankful for his car's interior cocoon feeling. *My living and thinking space for this awful duty.* Still, and quite annoyingly—even so protected from outside forces and physically fairly comfortable, when Ben looked down at his lap, he needed to brush away fine granules of yellowish sand from along the crease of his meticulously pressed right pants leg.

His leg-dusting action brought back his foul mood. Who should care that brilliant brushstroke-looking orange-red streaks appeared to surround him from all sides on the horizon? Indeed, if he squinted through the dust, even the Western horizon seemed aglow. A bowl-effect "weather phenomena" he figured, but still awesome if you're in the right mood. Which he clearly wasn't.

Not like yesterday morning.

He sighed again. Then he waited.

But Ben felt nothing change mood-wise. It was undeniable, though, his shift-duty-world *was* different this morning—and his psyche not only knew it, but also refused to let last night's impact go. *Hasn't affected me so strongly before.*

"I should feel elated. Am I changing?" he asked himself, and was startled by how loud his voice sounded inside his cruiser-cocoon. Ben stretched his long legs out a tad more, relieving some tension he wasn't previously aware of—and simultaneously noticed the air in his cruiser was becoming a little stale. But he dared not open a window to the dust-bowl outside his cocoon. He would just have to endure stuffiness for a bit.

"Wind is what's doing it." How easy it was to just blame his foul mood on the dust-laden winds.

Ben's words—spoken and in thought—were often selected and tempered by his self-image as a "gentleman" in the way his Uncle Gordon had defined the term. An image that even at this stage of his life, Ben still translated into a prohibition against using foul language to describe the many "situations" he found himself in. Mostly while on duty. He often had a hard time even *thinking*, much less *saying* off-color words—or heaven forbid, real curse words. For sure, he would never use the pejorative and ribald locker-room phrases sometimes used for describing sitting on your butt for hours and hours monitoring traffic in construction zones.

However, after further thought about his current circumstance, he did allow himself in thought, an additional, *this sucks*. Well, it did suck. Even with the knowledge this was supposedly his last shift day out here in the boonies. *And even with last night's success.*

In contrast to his lanky body, Ben's face was broad and full—and he puffed-up his substantial cheeks and blew out a walloping lung full of air; another unconscious mannerism, which at this point in his life, was a well-incorporated part of his emotional aspect. Usually a release leading him on to further thought.

Of course mornings aren't my thing. Not really. Even with these sunrise colors. A "night owl" was what he considered himself. Enjoying a dramatic sunset, then operating in the darkness was more to his liking. There was an "electrifying mystique" about the camouflage effects of darkness. The distortions to reality. Though being a kind of caretaker—which is

3

how he occasionally described himself in his chosen occupations—time requirements were always unpredictable, day and night. Like this morning.

There now was a heightening noise level from the din of gravel-spreading trucks, ground-leveling pounders, and water-sprinkling tanks—all pulling into the median in quick succession. Ben sighed yet again, more normally this time, and without his characteristic blowout of air. Then he slid his hand into his front pants pocket and unconsciously fingered his lucky medal with *Facit Justitia* engraved on it. He'd gotten it as a child from a machine in a museum his parents dragged him to somewhere in Europe. *England, I think.* Unfortunately, he couldn't remember the museum's name—but the machine making and dispensing the coins—he'd never forget. Ben even remembered the scenery and weather—a childhood memory of green, gentle breeze-touched European hills. Which brought him back to his self-proclaimed mantra this morning, *darned desert.*

From nowhere it seemed, his chest suddenly felt tight. Hard to breathe, almost. Indeed, he wanted to roll down his window again—but right now and here, in this site's dust-bowl environ, opening his window would be even worse for him. *Respiratory death.*

Dust, dust, and more dust. Now, Ben thought he could even taste dirt.

I wonder if I've really annoyed Captain Austin somehow? On the public-safety side of the coin, his actual law-enforcement bailiwick—with all the forewarning highway signs Caltrans had put up, and the real-world forced speed moderation from having to follow slower-moving semi-truck traffic—most heavy-footed auto drivers were forced to slow down. Consequently, Ben knew infractions would be minimal. *Of course* there would be a couple fools who would ignore all the warnings, *usually red sports cars.* He smiled at his own prejudiced thought about the color red—for Ben's personal automobile was a bright red Chevy pickup truck.

Adding insult to injury, out of nowhere, a particularly strong wind-driven swirling mixture of reddish-clay and sand-colored dust assaulted his windshield. First head-on—then wickedly sidling across the glass like a mass of dirt moving with intent. After its initial attack, the dust-glob offended further as it vortexed around his vehicle. *My poor FLIR camera and license reader are getting a walloping.* He knew from past experience, state-of-the-art high-tech equipment was only usable when in good working condition.

Ben's mind, emotions, and body were thus occupied when right in front of him—only thirty or so feet from where he was parked—a highway worker came charging out of the man-sized clay culvert they had previously lowered into place.

"A dead man, a dead man," the silhouette in front of him was yelling; while charging forward like a wild man, with one hand frantically grabbing at his orange high-visibility vest as if it were toxic, and waving his other arm in the air to get attention.

At first sight and hearing, the apparition-like figure's words were barely discernible given all the clatter, but Ben understood what was happening. *Knew* what was happening.

The worker was heading straight toward his Dodge Charger Pursuit black and white cruiser. Once close enough, Ben could see the worker was yelling directly at him, using barely comprehensible words, "I fell on him, I fell on him." He definitely wanted to get Ben's attention—and the attention of the rest of the orange-vest-clad "Sunrise" crew.

For Ben, and for just a flash, everything—men, trucks, noise—all seemed to stop. Pause. *As if Time itself blinked.* And in those few silent and surreal micro-seconds—even given the distance remaining between them—Ben felt his own eyes lock directly into the workman's wide-open large dark eyes. An impossible visual connection it would seem, given their dust-blown environment, but for a moment they were connected by "something" emanating directly to him from the workman's eyes—like a psychic laser-beam.

Far more than just surprise, the worker's eyes emanated that special revulsion few will ever experience. *He can't believe what he's just seen.* Ben had walked in similar shoes, reeled through similar emotions. Far more times than he now wanted to count.

Even with that recognition and connection, *even with* the suddenness and rapidity of happenings, and *even with* the noise and visibility issues—only seconds passed before Ben was dealing with his present reality, assessing the situation, and readying himself to take action. No matter all the crew were now also converging upon him—barely allowing his conscious mind time to complete what he knew from years of training and experience was needed. It was not exactly like the situation he expected, but Ben felt he could deal with it.

Then—on top of all the "happenings" outside, and almost simultaneously with the drama unfolding before him, Ben caught in the farthest corner of his peripheral vision "10-33" flashing on the screen of his state-of-the-art console dominating his center dash and gear box.

Then his radio beeped.

Then his cell phone rang.

Even with everything breaking loose at the same time—using his innate logistic competence developed over years of experience—Officer Ben Bellaeu managed to quickly and quite accurately assess his situation, and then act. With the press of one cell phone button, he speed-dialed a fellow officer in Shiné. A very competent Chief of Police he knew, albeit now holed-up in a small podunk town. Ben knew immediate decisions needed to be made, actions needed to be taken, and *competence* was required.

Fast.

Ben's radio and flashing console text were also both now "yelling" at him the same message—he needed to get to Cajon Pass immediately. *Ten-car crash, getting larger, pass shut down.* Now his heart was pounding rapidly. Though time was short, as best he could, Ben tried taking a readying deep slow breath.

All the while outside his cruiser, the yelling arm-waving DOT worker—now surrounded by a loud and chaotic rolling cloud-like scene of his fellow workers, also yelling and arm waving, were all descending upon his cruiser. A scene dramatized by continuing ear shattering equipment noise, and air-clogging desert dust swirling around them.

Not exactly how this shift should be starting. Ben had thought he would have some time to think before all hell broke loose.

"Yes, I'll dump my culvert dead body on Glover," Ben affirmed his on-the-fly decision aloud. When actually hearing his thoughts in the real world, he recognized his unintentional "body dumping" pun for what it was seconds after uttering the words. *Not a gentlemanly comment. Vulgar actually,* he thought in homage to his long deceased mother. Good or bad, there was a life gone — *a dead body dumped in the culvert*—and he was part of the whole thing. Not a joke or subject for a thoughtless remark.

"Then I'll call Needles. Get the county involved." He was speed dialing while talking to himself—and an expression of calmness slowly spread across his broad-featured oval face.

I can handle this, Ben reaffirmed—even though as if mocking him—flying all around the entire worksite was *dust, dust, and more dust.* Mother Nature trying to bury one more dead body in the desert.

"Not this time," Ben argued back at Her. "*This* culvert body has been found."

Still Saturday Morning: John Wayne Airport, Santa Ana, CA

Back to the damn desert again, Mugs Nightshade bemoaned as he left the Level O Kiosk to locate his airport rental car.

Not that he didn't like traveling. *Hell,* travel was often the most enjoyable part of the job. In today's case, his flights from the Midwest to California had been uneventful. Relaxing even.

Especially since he always flew first class and had room to stretch out. And Mugs liked John Wayne airport in Santa Ana.

This time he'd dressed for the southern California climate. Not layered in Midwest keep-the-weather-out clothes like before. Even remembered to bring shorts this time. "Fall" in southern California was not the same as "fall" in Chicago.

Indeed, as he headed toward his rental as directed by the attendant, Mugs was quite comfortable weather-wise. *Seventy-five maybe? Nice blue sky.* And he wasn't able to detect any of that smog stuff everyone was always going on about in Southern California. He took a deep breath of non-smog air, and for several moments actually took in the world around him. The sun was barely up, and he couldn't quite make out from the terminal complex what the horizon actually looked like—but he figured it was nice. "Maybe I could get used to this California living." Then his memory reminded him, quickly and sharply, *Santa Ana is not Shiné.*

He shuddered. *Damn desert.*

Mug's thoughts immediately returned to the whys and what-fors of his trip. He'd been hired by a client for a fix. And said client had dubbed him, "The Caretaker?" *What the hell did that mean?* He guessed it was like the janitor in his uncle's building back in Chicago. Kept the furnace going and toilets plunged? But he didn't think his client was calling him a janitor. *Was she?* No, Mugs definitely was going to stick with "The Fixer." She could keep the "caretaker" moniker.

He was pulling his roller-bag-suitcase with his left hand, and with his right, was still able to reflexively smooth the skin around his mouth and chin. Even though Mug's thoughts weren't completely happy, he was surprised to feel a slight upturn to the corners of his mouth. *A smile,* he wondered?

Probably not, given *where* he was ultimately traveling to. Big problem. One he would of course handle—*I'm known for my adaptability.* Be that as it may be, Mugs had sworn to himself to never take another fixer-job out in the stupid Mojave Desert. In particular, nowhere near the stretch around that no-nothing-town, with that crumbling chimney, stupid castle, and loony-toons out in the desert. Though in his mind, he was not only *The Fixer*, but also a good guy doing a necessary service. And the Mojave Desert was where the job was taking him.

Still, he certainly didn't want to go back to that god-awful desert. And on top of that, his target was a woman. He didn't like the woman part at all. *Not one bit.* Nonetheless, the "professional" Mugs Nightshade needed to take care of things, fix what was wrong—*regardless of gender.* On top of that, Mugs didn't feel he was in a position to refuse any job, and keep on breathing himself. *Damn, damn, and double-damn.*

After having finally identified and quickly looked over his rental car—*white again,* Mugs emotionally accepted what he was about to do. *Have to do.* He also pointed out to himself, the very reputation he built as a competent fixer—was the main reason he was out here in California. Especially with his seeming success last spring. Taking out Johnny Max when the first fixer Alex disappeared, had further cemented his reputation as a go-to Fixer.

Remembering, Mugs smiled as he conjectured about what island paradise he thought Alex was hiding out on. He figured Alex had just decided to get out of the business while he could.

In fact, it still amazed Mugs how that ditsy broad Mary Jones took out Johnny for him—pushing him over her balcony. Then how that film crew found "The Book," along with what he thought was Anthony L's body, and how the wind had subsequently taken Tony's insurance policy and blown it away across the sand dunes forever. Recalling those circumstances, and still smiling, Mugs also unconsciously nodded his head. *All the while those stupid people making a movie about Route 66, and that keystone-cop and his buddy trying to catch me.*

"Route Sixty-Six," he said aloud and blew out his cheeks. Mugs had definitely liked watching that TV show back in the sixties. Usually over at his grandmother's on Paulina Street.

"What's to complain about, anyway?" he reassured himself aloud about his current circumstances. With easy flights into Vegas, then on to Santa Ana, and finally just a couple hours drive to *that* town. *Smart,* choosing to fly to LA area first from Vegas, then drive to the desert. *Longer,* but not as easily traceable. *I'm a sly one.* Then, all he had to do was find the woman. His escape plan was to leave from Santa Ana, too. *They'll never guess.*

Still, not liking the thought or taste of this whole job— Mugs tried bringing up favorable memories. Ones he could enjoy during the ride out into no-man's land. Like the nightshade along his grandmother's alley chain link fence.

For the Mugs Nightshade he knew and accepted, wasn't completely insensitive to heart-tugging sentimentality. In fact, in many respects he considered himself an average man—*a regular ole Joe.* And not just when it came to "human sensitivities," but also physical things like his height, build, and his neither ugly nor handsome features. For sure, his left-handedness and slender fingers were his most distinguishing features. *And my hair,* he occasionally also reflected; still thick like Uncle Harry's, and still jet black with help from his barber Leo. He smiled at the thought of his thick black hair. Kind of a trademark.

But those movie people. Mug's thoughts unfortunately returned to his last occasion to visit the Mojave. *I just got out in time.* From this same airport, he remembered with a returning smile in appreciation of his smarts and cunning.

Pressing the door-unlock button on his rental key fob and finding it didn't work, Mugs put the attached latest-styled slender key in the lock of his white Altima rental. It worked, and he sighed with relief. *Won't have to go all the way back and get a replacement.*

Once again he took a deep breath. The air still smelled clean, refreshing, and hopefully a good deep breath would keep him from going back down his woe-is-me path. Quite easily, Mugs let his mind and emotions take him in a different direction—back to his *special memory.*

Indeed, a memory he could seldom control, surfaced full-blown in his mind's eye. It was a picture-memory, which even at this stage of his life, still appeared most vividly. A picture-memory of flowering purple nightshade growing on his grandmother's chain link fence along the alley. *A long time ago. Me a kid on Paulina Street.* For Mugs, those days still persisted as purple and green nightshade-embossed pictures—popping up as they did, seemingly willy-nilly. But he had loved his grandmother deeply, and his subconscious evidently would never forget her colorful out-of-control nightshade. *Never.*

Regrettable to Mugs, once finally sitting in his rental's bucket seat, his mind reverted back to aggravation-mode as he searched for the seat-slider lever. Paulina Street was returned to its proper memory slot.

"Good grief," Mugs complained aloud while searching for his rental's seat lever. In its current position, he was barely close enough to press the brake or gas pedal halfway down, much less to the floor. *Must have been a giant driving this car before me.*

An observation which reminded him of the missing-in-action Noiseless Killer—*reputed to be a giant of a man by all who had met him..* Another fixer gone missing. "What's with this damn desert anyway?"

Saturday Morning: On California I-40 approaching exit heading North to Shiné

Adeleine Moore was feeling the need for a bathroom. *Again.*

And given how tired she was from traveling—even though in the lap-of-luxury in the back compartment of their outlandishly appointed limousine, with its tinted windows, sound proofing, and controlled air purification system—she found it mentally and emotionally incomprehensible how human beings ever made the journey westward. Even with modern day rest stop conveniences and cafés, she was definitely wearing out.

Made of tougher stuff than me. "I can't imagine how they did it."

"Did what?" her father Winston asked from his side of their plush backseat.

She was surprised he heard her, and even more amazed he responded with a question. "How they made this journey we're making. Settled all this land."

Land—most of which after leaving Missouri looked and felt foreign to her. Not that Adeleine hadn't traveled at all, but only eastward in the US, and "across the pond" to Europe.

Nothing like this.

"Must have been extremely difficult back then." She mentally tried putting herself in the place of early settlers. Way before the interstate, earlier even before Route 66 came about. Though her imagination couldn't take her to the mental place where she could "walk in their shoes"—her heart felt for them in a vague empathetic sort of way.

Winston brought his eyes up from the work-related tome on top of his portable-lap-desk, to look out his window for half a minute at the passing scenery. "Malcolm can tell you where we are," he said, in his trip-long disinterest for the scenery tone. His eyes went back to his papers—where Adeleine surmised, his real attention never actually left.

She knew he was making this trip to protect her—though she didn't know much more. Her father had so far refused to share important details. But Adeleine *did* know they were "on the run," to use TV language. More accurately, looking for a place for her to hide out. *Funny, I'm not really that scared. Maybe I should be....*

With a sigh directed at her father's disinterest in her thoughts, his deviousness, her lack of fear, and her lack of understanding of how "they" had survived the journey westward in the past—Adeleine pulled out her Route 66 road guide. She had sporadically watched the signs, and based on

Malcolm and her father's meager dispensing of travel information, she thought they might be nearing their destination. She certainly hoped so.

Even though Adeleine figured their chauffeur was quite tired of her constant pit-stops, she reached over to the intercom button that connected them with their driver. She would ask Malcolm to please stop at the next rest area.

But first, before actually electronically connecting with Malcolm—having gotten used to the diffusion properties of tinted glass, and liking how it mellowed the world outside— Adeleine looked out her window to see if by some miracle, a sign would pop up for an upcoming rest area.

What she saw were what looked like swirling funnels of sand rolling by a turnoff road sign. She shivered, physically and mentally.

Even though she was diminutive in stature and girth, *like my mother*, Winston must have noticed her body movements, and looked up long enough to ask, "Are you alright?"

Adeleine nodded, and Winston Moore went back to his papers.

Amazing people, those early travelers, she thought anew.

Chapter Two
Foul Play from the Start

From LC's journal: Some things are important, and sometimes you just got to take care of them things. I know the world is a going to change. But I need to make sure things change the way I'm wanting them to. That traveling lawyer said there's words can go in the deeds. Going to do that. Cause in building this town, I've learned folks see things from their own perspective. Viola says real nice like what I know to be true. "Where you stand on wanting something, LC, oftentimes depends on where you're already sitting."

Still Saturday Morning : Across the road from Rhodes Castle

"Damn," Walker Johns cursed. A strong word for him, but circumstances were extreme. He also knew whatever he might say would be muffled by his thermal mask—and no one was close enough to hear him anyway.

Ambulance Technician and occasional stand-in deputy for Chief of Police Glover Deers—Walker was also one of five Shiné and environs volunteer firefighters. During his tenure of wearing these various hats of responsibility, Walker had unfortunately built up more unpleasant experiences than he would have wished. His callouts had even included assisting other fire departments with incidents in nearby High Desert communities. But *this* was the first "really big" blaze he'd been tapped out for.

This is awful.

Unfortunately, he'd lost track of the time, and was beginning to feel in-over-his-head on several fronts—wondering about reinforcements, and in particular, would his body and mental stamina be good enough to actually help?

Who else could be coming? Just plain logistic support sure would be helpful. *And where the heck is Leiv or The Chief?* Sure, Rhodes Castle was set back from the road, but up high a bit, and he figured the flames must be visible for miles. *Leiv should be seeing this by now? And what about the smell?*

Nothing like the odor of desert plants smoldering—even dirt seemed to emanate an odor during a fire. *Makes me want to gag even with my mask.* Especially with the gusts of wind whipping through this morning, stirring up everything it could into its clutches. *Well,* maybe Glover was on his way. *Must have been called by now.* They didn't use codes like 10-13 or 904 much anymore, but the word had indeed been sent out to all agencies by now—and in plain English.

Fire!

Lucca's doublewide hadn't seemed like much before, just like all the others out here—until engulfed in fire as it now was, a modest home had become a monstrous fire.

Awful. But we got Lucca out at least.

In his peripheral vision, Walker could see Mark—one of his fellow paramedics-cum-firefighters working over the caretaker's prone body. Sadly, Lucca looked more like a life-sized dummy splayed awkwardly on a patch of Mojave Desert scrubland. *Like the wind had just tossed his body there.*

He could see some of Mark's Personal Protection Equipment—helmet, gloves, camera, radio, mask, and box light, all strewn on the ground next to the young firefighter as he performed CPR on Lucca. Walker also caught sight of their unit's defibrillator on the ground next to them. *At the ready.* Walker's instinct was to run over and help with resuscitating Leiv Rhodes's caretaker, but his firefighter brain knew he was needed for hose duty. *Mark knows what he's doing.* And Walker figured he could still keep an eye on them. *Well, maybe not if this fire gets any worse.*

For the first time since his arrival at least half an hour ago, Mark noticed and felt the sweat pouring down his sides under his seventy-plus pounds of turnout gear. He considered his stamina rather good, and prided himself on being a physically fit young man, with a sturdy enough build and well-proportioned for carrying gear. He also knew to keep well-hydrated during on-call times. Still, *this is awful,* he reaffirmed yet again. And his initial doubts about being able to meet the challenge flashed for a second time. *No time for more introspection now.*

Shiné's Quint fire truck had arrived onsite first, then an E-One truck followed—he wasn't sure from where, but guessed Baker environs. Once on scene in response to the 911 call, they started with a booster hose, then moved up to a crosslay.

The sickly smoke smell, intense heat, and wind flashing the flames were intense from the start—requiring his little band of volunteer firefighters to immediately tackle the blaze with whatever they could. And as always, out in this part of the desert, there was the limited water pressure and relentless winds. Despite all their efforts so far, Lucca's place remained ablaze. Not just smoldering, but real oxygenating billowing flames.

Damn fire. Damn winds.

Suddenly, Walker felt dead tired—as if a wave of fatigue blanketed him. His sweating moved to sweltering underneath all the PPE Fire Chief Parnell insisted they wear. Walker knew it was from pushing himself physically and mentally—what with the hoses, the uneven terrain, the blasts of wind thwarting their every move, and frequent lapses in visibility. But knowing didn't make any of it better.

So far, assisting with a ten car pileup a couple years back on I-15 had been his worse experience. Bad burns that time—*a mangled and dead body even.* But he had never before experienced the exhaustion and helplessness trying to overcome him now. He fancied for a second he could see in his mind's eye his heart beating in his chest. Hear it thumping in his inner ear. *Hallucinating?*

Then just as suddenly, the blaze changed—color, velocity, intensity—different.

Diminishing?

Glover's cell phone rang, annoying Leiv on several fronts.

First off, he'd asked Shiné's Chief of Police to turn the darned thing off.

Secondly, they were in the middle of a *special* breakfast at The Greasy Spoon, fondly referred to as TGS. And, quite comfortably seated in the special "hideout booth," as Glover's mother Margaret Deers dubbed it one morning—almost a year past now. The booth was the last seating available, way in the back, near the door to the restrooms. Most TGS patrons did not want to occupy *that* particular booth, nor cared who did.

Tucked away as they were this morning was perfect for what Leiv wanted to talk to Glover about. He guessed the wind was still howling outside, but you certainly wouldn't know it back in Margaret's hideout booth. *No,* here he planned on having Glover to himself. Consequently, when Glover's phone intrusively rang, Leiv was not only physically well situated in TGS, but also emotionally primed for spilling the Mojave-Stone beans—his main reason in asking Glover to breakfast.

Of course, he knew they first needed to start in on their platters of French toast before getting to the heart of his intended conversation. French toast was not on TGS's menu, but was being specially prepared for them by Chef Jack—at Leiv's personal request—for this morning's heart-to-heart with his brother via a shared father. Once they were eating, Leiv thought, the mood would be relaxed and Glover would better understand why he'd kept the Mojave-Stone secrets to himself for so long.

Now Glover's damn phone has rung. Spoiling everything.

Further irritating Leiv, Glover looked down at his phone sitting on the table and asked the contraption, "What's up?"—as if it were a person before actually picking it up and answering.

Leiv continued to fume mildly, even resorting to squinting his already thin eyes even more—a technique he used in his past life on prosecutors and defense attorneys alike whom he found irritating. Forcing his eyes into little slits made his other facial features seem even more disproportionate than they already were—producing what he called his evil-eye glare. Glover however, turned his head toward the kitchen door while answering his cell phone, consequently nullifying Leiv's tactic.

He doesn't dare look at me. Knows he shouldn't be answering the thing because it shouldn't have rung.

Leiv almost clicked out the side of his mouth—but caught himself in time. He especially didn't want Glover to realize that like their new friend, film producer Charlie White—he was also picking up one of Glover's western-styled mannerisms. *Funny that, Glover and his iconic mannerisms. Even funnier,* he further thought, *our wanting to emulate a silly clicking sound out the side of our mouths.*

He had made a point of asking Glover to breakfast *away from* the Shiné Police office *and to turn his phone off* before they started eating. So what if he was on duty? They were in Shiné for goodness' sake.

Okay, so they had already seen over the last year or so more than their share of bad happenings. *Especially murders.* Leiv figured a quiet period had to be in the offing. Just because Glover was in uniform and lugging along his official campaign hat didn't mean "something" *had* to happen. Indeed, Leiv expected this morning to be quiet. A perfect time to talk about Mojave Stones.

Admittedly, when Leiv was still "On the Bench" back in

Illinois, a running observation—usually brought up at some late night poker games after too much booze—was how criminal activity seemed to come in waves. Especially with some of the more heinous variety. If a really bad case came up, then you'd be sure several would soon follow. And if you kept up on Prosecutor and Grand Jury activity for all the judges and combined arraignment reports—the patterns just seemed to jump out at you. *Except for Judge Kelvin Altrue.* He was always surprised when a run of crap-cases came his way. Leiv almost smiled remembering the most clueless judge he'd ever known. *Yet unbelievably lucky at poker.*

Leiv pulled his thoughts back to Glover, and his sustained annoyance caused him to next rub his chin with the back of his right hand, and was surprised by the haphazard, though very light stubble he felt. Evidently, this was such an important breakfast for him, in his haste to arrive on time he hadn't shaved properly.

He sighed loudly, accompanied by a disgusted-sounding puff of air. He had finally decided to tell Glover about the Mojave Stones. A big deal for sure. Especially in light of the adventures they shared this last year—combined with the friendship based on trust and confidence they were developing. *And us having the same father.*

But now, after only half-a-minute on the phone—before Leiv could express his ire, much less launch into a lengthy and chastising explanation for the purpose of this special breakfast— Glover stood up, quickly tossed a twenty on the table and started making movements indicating he was leaving.

In exiting their booth area, Glover did manage to smile at Leiv, but with a facial expression clearly saying his mind was elsewhere. "Sorry. I know you wanted to tell me something, but I gotta go."

Leiv continued to watch in amazement as Glover's expression next turned grave before he sucked in a lengthy drag of air—then let it out in a long, slow exhalation. All making

Glover's solidly-built tough-guy persona, with his usually stoic countenance, seem uncharacteristically unsettled and concerned. Somehow, it made Glover seem even more formidable. *Curious.*

And why wasn't Glover cluing him in on what was happening? Especially if it was something so bad.

Then two thoughts, aberrant and unrelated to what was happening, flitted through Leiv's mind. The first, *he's put on his John Wayne face to go with his hat,* and the other, more personal and emotion-laden, *he's looking more like our father as he gets older.*

When looking at Glover, handsome almost, and solid for sure—it still often took Leiv by surprise when he reminded himself that they were the same height, and probably close in weight. But so different in personas. In contrast to Glover, he thought his own facial features, bland and rather subdued, tended more toward his mother Sophie.

Not that Leiv was complaining—his occasional evil eye notwithstanding— his own looks and persona were helpful in his past life as a judge. Particularly when he needed to blend into the background, or appear to be an impartial mediator. *Not so helpful* on the occasions when a command-performance had been called for. But he had managed. *Fairly well, if the fawners and suck-ups were to be believed.*

"What's happened?" Leiv's words, when he finally spoke to an in-motion Glover, sounded perfunctory to his own ears. For once, and for the moment, his curiosity toward police business was not a priority. *I want to tell you about the stones.*

Glover finally turned his attention directly to Leiv, "Dead body in a culvert on I-40 right at our Shiné exit."

Leiv felt his eyes widen. All his apathy gone. Couldn't help it. "Mysterious dead bodies again?" *Now I am interested. A murder?* "Near Dad's? But—" Leiv's own phone rang, interrupting and startling him, even causing him to jump a little—for he thought he'd turned it off.

Here I am, as bad as Glover.

21

Consequently, before Leiv could say or do more, Glover took the opportunity to make his getaway a reality. The Chief had yet to remove his heavy bomber-style jacket that matched his dark blue pants, and consequently was able to make his escape in just a few more seconds—without further time needed for gathering stuff, comment, or ado.

Leiv sighed, dug his *own* offending cell from the pocket of his *own* jacket on the booth bench seat next to him. The ID said Pastor Apply, but it certainly was an odd time for him to be calling. "Hello, Lloyd?"

"We're on our way, the Doc and me."

Leiv didn't have a clue what Lloyd was talking about. Maybe the body on I-40 Glover just mentioned? But surely, that was police business.

The pastor didn't wait for him to catch-up, "Right across the road from your place." Before Leiv could push for more understanding, his friend hung up.

Mojave Stone revelations to Glover were immediately and completely forgotten—his curiosity grabbed by Lloyd's cryptic call. Now with his own sense of urgency and alacrity akin to what Glover had displayed, Leiv stood up, grabbed his jacket, and dropped another twenty on the table just as he saw Chef Jack heading their way with a confused look on his face.

Leiv stopped himself. The best chef he had ever met deserved an explanation. Eventually, after several moments of explanation and discussion, he also left TGS—but with a container stuffed with French toast he knew was better than any he could ever prepare. *And* an ice-block in a bag for him to set it on. *Chef Jack is a jewel.* Leiv thought the ice a particularly thoughtful gesture, even though fall was full-blown, with desert temperatures dropping daily. Though, as Chef Jack clearly knew, it could still get hot as the day progressed.

Once in the parking lot heading to his pickup, out of nowhere, Leiv's stomach flip-flopped—not so much from hunger and thinking about his French toast—but because he instinctively knew *something* was starting he knew nothing about.

Once again, since his return to Shiné, *something* unanticipated was happening in his little world. *Something* he couldn't prepare for—even guess at. *Once again,* danger—maybe even evil awaited. He pushed down a shudder that followed his stomach harbinger, while simultaneously feeling a smile spreading across his face—quite incongruent with his apprehensive thoughts and bodily reactions. And definitely not under his control. For along with, and despite his growing sense of foreboding, "stuff" was happening—and he found himself feeling excited.

"And across from my place," he murmured, as a surprisingly chilly and dust-laden blast of wind from the west slammed Leiv, and took his words eastward as soon as he spoke them. But despite a Mojave wind blast catching him unawares, Leiv's thoughts and intentions started taking on more form. Whatever was going on, good or bad—either way, he wanted to be involved. A definite attitude change from just moments earlier.

Leiv stopped and looked up to the east for a moment. The brilliance of the morning sunrise as he drove into Shiné and TGS had almost dissipated—leaving a peachy glow in its wake. Dreamsicle orange.

But he didn't have time to hang around admiring sunrises, and quickly climbed into his dark-blue Ford pickup. Once seated, Leiv did allow thoughts from his lawyer and judge days to intrude again for a moment. Both periods had been jam-packed with surprises and intrigues. *Almost entirely political.* But in these last several Shiné years, leaving all that legal and political "stuff" behind, Leiv returned to his father and grandfather's legacy town and castle-home off Route 66, for peace and quiet he'd thought. Then unexpectedly, his new Mojave surroundings and desert-life ended up surprising him in many different ways.

Mentally and physically. *Mojave Stones intrigues. Murders. Finding a brother.*

Indeed, as Leiv prepared to pull out of TGS's modest gravel parking lot, but before actually heading south—he again smiled slightly while reminiscing about his last "adventure," and in particular, the movie-making crew he was now friends with. One of them, David Milhouse, was about to marry his former housekeeper, Hester Miller, next week. *Still hard to believe that.* He shook his head, but continued to smile.

Leiv carefully set his French toast on the floor in front of the passenger seat, then turned on his motor.

The crew-member in particular who had captured Leiv's imagination was Pete Lily. The photographer. Not that he actually wanted to hop in a helicopter and actually *fly* over Shiné and hang over the side of the noisy contraption and film—like Pete had done several times. *No,* seeing Shiné only by car or on foot was for sure a circumstance unlikely to change. Involuntarily, he shuddered at the thought of getting in a helicopter.

Yet, the idea of being able to see the area from above, see what was going on, who was where and doing what—was still captivating, and continued to grab at his imagination. *What a perspective on our little world.* Though Leiv doubted one could actually see close-up stuff from helicopter level. *Maybe?* But a bird's eye view no matter the level of detail would be great for sure.

If only Melissa were still alive to share with me.... He quickly banished the intruding emotion with its accompanying grief. "Not now."

Leiv turned on his signal light, *as if there were any traffic in Shiné*—and finally pulled out of TGS's parking lot onto the two-lane paved road. He needed to move toward whatever lay ahead down the road.

"What I really need out here in the Mojave is precognition. *Know* what's going to happen before it happens."

Then he thought he saw a plume of smoke rising way down the road. *Near Rhodes Castle?*

Then Leiv thought he smelled smoke.

But before he could logically process all these happenings and thoughts bombarding him, simultaneously and seemingly out of nowhere—considering Leiv's last contact with Chef Jack—the chef himself, driving his pride-and-joy Jaguar, slowed to a moving stop in the road next to his pickup. He was in passing position on the two-way road, heading south just like Leiv.

Bewildered, Leiv quickly looked to his passenger seat floor—as if seeing his to-go box laden with French toast would reaffirm the sequence of recent happenings. *Yes, I did just leave Chef Jack in the TGS.* Yet within minutes, the Chef was there, now next to him, alone and driving his own car. Had he closed TGS? *Didn't have time, did he?*

The Jag's passenger side window lowered, Chef Jack leaned slightly across his center shift-column, and yelled out at Leiv, "What's taking you so long?"

Leiv was stupefied.

"Becca just called," Chef Jack continued excitedly. "She's already there." Then his window went back up, and within another second, he'd gunned his Jag's engine—three-hundred plus horse power, or more, *Leiv guessed*—and sped out ahead of him at a dangerously high speed.

It took Leiv a moment to realize his mouth was open, his jaw dropped. But after pulling himself together, he headed south, too—in his beloved Ford truck, which now felt inadequately gutless. Nonetheless, he was also driving at a speed well over the limit. *Not that gutless.*

After a few moments of driving, he was able to pinpoint the emotion this morning's circumstances and Chef Jack's departure had started churning up. He had felt a similar anxiety and alarm-bell alertness at this level five years or so ago—when the friend of a three-time-loser had pulled a gun in his courtroom.

"But now I'm in Shiné," he told himself aloud. Leiv sighed and pushed his gas pedal to the floor with resolve.

At first sight by Walker Johns, Jasmine Fabero looked like an ethereal floating blur as she ran towards them. He was squatting on the ground next to his compatriot Mark, who was trying to resuscitate the soot-encrusted body of Lucca Fabero. Walker had removed his helmet, facemask, and breather—but his eyes had yet to refocus correctly. He knew from experience it would take a few seconds, but at this moment of first seeing Jasmine—it almost felt like he was looking at an apparition.

Now, he could see her gait was more stumbling than running, and both her hands were grabbing at her face. Her jeans, T-shirt, and shoes were encrusted with soot and dirt just like her father Lucca Fabero. *An apparition alright.* But up close—dirty, disheveled, and probably in shock—not a particularly alluring picture.

Walker had seen victim shock and pain reactions before, but this time it was especially gut-wrenching. He knew her, and was a bit smitten, he knew; consequently not having an appropriate verbal response he could draw upon caused Walker to feel quite inadequate.

I seldom do in times of tragedy. A definite failing, he thought, for a first responder of any type. The reality of *wanting* to comfort a victim, and then being able to do so, were quite different personality attributes. He didn't think he possessed both.

In a few more seconds, Jasmine was close enough for Walker to hear anguish and fear in her voice—she was yelling, or, more like screaming her words—and sounding incredulous. "He must be just sleeping. Just sleeping...."

Minutes earlier, Walker had asked Mark a similar question. "Is he just passed out?"

Now next to them, Jasmine dropped to her knees on the ground by Walker, again repeating several times, "Is he just sleeping?" She started to lean over—looking like she was going to get in Mark's way trying to hug her father—but Walker instinctively wrapped his arm around her shoulders and pulled her back. *I need to take care of her.*

Another moment passed wherein no one spoke, no one moved. Silent. Suddenly calm. Unreal.

Finally, and even though Mark didn't look sideways at Walker or Jasmine, he was speaking to them directly—his tone laden with palpable pain as he said the dreaded words, "Lucca's gone."

Walker wanted to yell, to cry, pound his hands against something—anything. He couldn't scream out his disbelief and pain like Jasmine had. He was doing a job. An important job. *I'm a grownup Ambulance Technician, firefighter, Assistance Deputy. I don't cry, now do I? Can't show how I really feel, can I?*

But regardless of what Walker Johns, "volunteer extraordinaire," thought his grownup self should do in the real world, he found himself pushing-in-closer to Lucca's side—then pounding on the prone man's chest like a petulant child. "No, no!" Walker demanded of the world. "Not Lucca, not Lucca."

Everything and everyone else disappeared. It was just him and Lucca. He pounded on the old man's chest again. *Then* again. He couldn't help himself.

Then—Lucca's manikin-looking body sat straight up, coughed roughly—sounding more like a wretch—turned his eyes to Walker and said, "What's happened?"

Sitting inside his truck on the west side of the road for some very long moments—engine off, feeling not actually parked, but definitely stopped—Leiv tried taking it all in. Visually and emotionally. But he just couldn't comprehend it all.

Too much. Just the same, he continued to stare at the scene across the road from Rhodes Castle's uphill driveway—trying to figure out what happened.

He had pulled up and stopped behind a makeshift fire line barricade made of hoses and wooden sawhorses. Slowly, his brain identified Doc Walker and Mary Jones standing at the barricade. Then next to them—*like in a lineup of friends*—were Pastor Apply, Elizabeth-May, Margaret Deers, Chef Jack, and his wife Becca. Most surprisingly, even Hermit Chan was there. All motionless. *Stunned like me?* Except for Mary, all lived south of Shiné—in fact, south of him—and must have heard or smelled the awfulness he was now trying to take in himself.

All this going on while I was agonizing over telling Glover about Mojave-Stones.

Leiv felt quite abashed it took him so long to realize something so big and awful was going on right across the road from his home. Thank goodness, he'd finally left TGS and driven—following as fast as he dared in Chef Jack's metaphorical dust—to where he now sat in his pickup next to the chef's Jaguar in a sludge-filled and rutted track. A track Leiv guessed, freshly created by big pieces of equipment like fire trucks. *Sand mud.*

He remained still for a bit longer, not yet able to internalize what he was taking in. *Especially* since a fire was not something Leiv expected in his desert environment. Especially considering the beautiful start to the morning he witnessed from Rhodes Castle's copula in the dawn-breaking hours. He had even taken some moments to marvel at the touch of orange starting to illuminate the horizon. Thinking, *its going to be a good day.* Especially since he anticipated a long awaited "Mojave Stone" unburdening morning with Glover.

Now this. Just across the road. And his friends knew about the fire before him. Ironic for sure. Evidently, his own resolve and anguish over telling Glover about the Mojave-Stones had overshadowed everything else. *Even my sense of smell?*

He shook his head. Of that, at least, Leiv was sure—*no*, the fire had not started before or while he left home for TGS in Shiné. Nonetheless, he felt self-incrimination at what he considered self absorption at the expense of others—most common in juveniles ending up in his court.

"I'm too old to be so tunnel-visioned." Indeed, he expected better of himself; but now was not the time for continued self-analysis as a windblown whiff of acrid soot-laden air invaded his truck cab. Leiv was instantly brought back to the awfulness on the property Lucien "Lucca" Fabero was caretaking for LC. He corrected himself—*caretaking for me.*

Leiv tried to focus more on the overall scene. From the sky to the earth he could see, a dark heavy grey-blackness enveloped the whole eastern side of the highway. He was able to make out enough details to see two fire trucks, loads of hoses, and Shiné's paramedic van. There were ruts everywhere—and in vague and ominous detail, the blackened fire-destroyed remains of Lucca's doublewide. *Lucca's home.*

On top of all that, just in the few moments Leiv sat in his truck taking it all in, the smoke-permeated air seemed to get thicker—with several dark billows even seeming to expand.

He forced himself to take a slow shallow breath—paying attention this time to the smoke-laden smells—incomprehensibly damp and dry at the same time. *Barely breathable, even inside my truck.* He reached to press his window-up button, but saw both his truck windows were already closed tight. He also noted an additional and unique desert smell he couldn't quite label. *Dirt doesn't burn, or smell, does it?* Whatever the odor, it brought an acrid taste to his mouth.

In this unpleasant world Leiv struggled to take in, he now also saw there were a surprising number of other people looking on that he hadn't noticed when first arriving at the awful scene. *From out of town? Off Route 66?* The smoke was probably visible from I-40 by now. It looked like some bystanders had even entered the fire zone area to help out as best they could. Leiv was quite surprised. Was his Shiné universe larger than his little Rhodes Castle world?

Amongst all his ricocheting thoughts, Leiv still managed to make a mental note to talk to Glover about what actually did comprise his Shiné police-world. *Possibly more than the Shiné LC cobbled together.* Even more puzzling—where were all these people when Johnny Max lay dead and alone on the pavement in front of Le Bric-à-Brac last spring? *There must be twenty-or-so people at this scene. None then.*

He didn't see Glover in the almost overwhelming collage spreading out before him. Then he remembered—a body on I-40.

Finally, even with the awful air quality his senses had already identified, Leiv took one of his regular long, slow, and supposedly calming breaths. *I used to be a judge for Christ's sake.* Immediately after which, Leiv realized that he couldn't just "breathe away" what his eyes had caught in the panorama before him. And the air was still barely breathable—causing him to cough painfully in response.

Then he finally saw his caretaker, Lucca Fabero, lying on the ground inside the barricades—right in front of him. Walker, another firefighter, and Lucca's daughter Jasmine were kneeling on the ground at his side.

No. No. Not Lucca. He felt his breath catch. *He can't be dead.*

He looked down at his hands which had tightened on his steering wheel to the point of pain. He relaxed them a bit, and tried to simultaneously bring his mind and emotions back under control. Then for a second, he felt a touch of the hot anger of outrage he'd sporadically felt during his first few years on the bench.

Rage, eventually brought under his control over the years. But evidently not completely vanquished.

He saw Jasmine trying to bend down over Lucca's body. Walker pulled her back, comforting her, it looked like.

Another moment or two passed during which Walker started pounding on Lucca's chest....

As Leiv continued struggling to get his body and mind in sync with circumstances, he started to get out of his truck to go help Walker—but as he turned to open his door, he caught in his peripheral vision a big black car coming toward him from the south.

A turn signal? Going up my drive? The vehicle actually did turn and started going up his driveway road. *A limousine?* In the smokey haze that was starting to now also envelop the west side of the road, he needed to squint his eyes to be certain. But *yes,* it was a real live limousine—*in Shiné of all the unbelievable places*—and heading up LC's grandiose driveway. Coming to see him? He couldn't imagine who or why?

The car, and seeing for sure it was a limousine, triggered Leiv's most familiar, uncontrollable, and seldom-requested memory. Though he fought back against his psyche, Leiv's mind and heart were out of his control as they transferred him back to that day in Chicago…

…*Hearing Melissa—her sweet words. "What a lovely evening." Her voice lilting and harmonic—a little bit of song always there.*

Chicago. Hundreds of thousands of cars drove on I-290 as it miraculously, it seemed, went under the Chicago Post Office. Yes, they were on the "Ike" that night, or the Congress Expressway, depending on your generation. He and Melissa knew it as the quickest way to head west and get out of the city.

It was fall, had rained all day, and an overcast night was engulfing the city. Leiv was tired, and figured Melissa was too. Hence the driver. Hence the limousine.

…the back of their limousine driver's head was vividly still in his memory. The front interior light must have been on. Why? A question he still didn't know the answer to.

Then waking up in the hospital, after a week in a coma, he was told. No memories until Melissa's sobbing sister at the side of his hospital bed told him she was dead. Then she'd slapped him, cursed him forever for meeting her sister.

I should have been driving. Not called for a car....

Leiv was jerked back to the present, and his jaw actually dropped open as he watched Lucca miraculously sit straight up. Then even more incredulous—especially from his distant position on his side of the sawhorse barricade, and inside his truck—Leiv heard the caretaker's voice clear as a bell, asking, "What's happened?"

Limousines, past and present, were immediately pushed into the background.

Today's limousine occupants would just have to wait until he got there. *Sit on the stoop,* he remembered words from his childhood. Right now, he needed to finally dislodge himself from his truck, go over to see Lucca and find out what had happened. The winds seemed even stronger than when he arrived. Blowing ash, sand, smoke—pushing against his door, swirling around from all sides. Leiv had seen such winds before, but still, *unnerving*.

He wished Glover were around to tell him what was going on—for he sure didn't know what was happening, but his reliable stomach harbinger—via several immediate and intense flip-flops—told him quite emphatically—*watch out*.

Adeleine Moore's mind still boggled at the vast uninhabited stretches she saw during their journey—and especially now, having turned off the interstate in scrub-desert territory. To her Midwest-acculturated eye, the barrenness of the Mojave was quite a visual shock—bringing with it an emotionality she was yet able to label. *Scary?* She rubbed her forehead and found it damp. *Shouldn't be,* given the actual temperature in their limousine. Malcolm had explained how their interior temperature, front and back, was automatically controlled.

And now, on top of all the new terrain and environments seen over their days on the road, and finally almost at journey's end—Adeleine was witness to a serious emergency event coming up to their right, just on the other side of the road of their final turnoff. In addition, there were awful smells invading their supposedly airtight cocoon, and an eerie darkness hung in the air—magnified no doubt by tinted glass. And quite ominous in look and emotional impact. *Smoke? Soot?*

Per Malcolm, Judge Rhodes's place should be up the road-like driveway to their left. And if her internal compass-bearings were still working after all the road twists and turns, they were now heading north, and were about to turn westerly—up a driveway lined with some kind of pine-like tree she'd never seen before. Though Adeleine thought she still retained her bearings on north and south, she wasn't sure *where* they were in the larger California-state scheme of things. *Hopefully we're "there" at last?*

Destination achieved or not, she still couldn't ignore the scene across the road, and the horrendous wind now buffeting even their substantial limo. Malcolm slowed down only enough to navigate the turn, then head up the road toward what Adeleine guessed was their destination. What she was able to take in as they turned and her visual vista changed—had looked like the aftermath of a fire. *In the desert?*

Her stomach flip-flopped, prompting her to ask her father, "Are you sure we're in the right spot?" She recognized apprehension and a touch of petulance edging her tone. *Still feel like a child with him sometimes.*

Silence.

Adeleine turned her head to look at him. Winston Moore seemed to be looking straight ahead. She mused, a side view was not the best perspective to view him, given his prominent nose. *Funny that.* For she knew he considered that very nose a point of distinction.

She was sure he had heard her—but even from her side view, his facial expression combined with his lack of a verbal response indicated his mind was once again elsewhere. Adeleine almost sighed, but didn't. *Machiavellian political plotting no doubt,* she further speculated. Unfortunately, a touch of long-seated ill will when it came to his political maneuverings and shenanigans accompanied her thought.

At the same time, Adeleine was long enured to her father's ways on many fronts, so she easily switched on the armrest-embedded intercom connecting them to the front of their limo—and without preamble, asked their driver the same question. "Malcolm, are you sure we're in the right place?"

"Yes, Ma'am," he said while smiling at her via his rearview mirror.

She philosophized, and not for the first time during their trip, *it's like talking to someone in another world.* The psychological aspect of a glass barrier was indeed thought provoking. Especially the lack of eye contact except through a rearview mirror added to what she dubbed, "limousine otherworldliness."

The limousine arrangement on whole was strange at first, but one she was now used to. *Chicago to California in a limo.* Although, the "whole thing" remained disconcerting—and definitely a story she hoped to retell far into the future. Her father had confided enough before they left Illinois for Adeleine to present their current predicament as dire. At the time, she thought he was exaggerating—but still....

Malcolm completed turning the relatively small black Cadillac limousine left and uphill—heading toward the unknown. Now the stands of large pine-like trees were thicker, and gave their simple driveway journey an unexpected mysteriousness—which in turn, pulled her attention from the fire into this new direction. What kind of place is this?

"Did you just say something, dear?" She heard her father finally mumble in a tone clearly indicating he was still not really listening, but didn't want to completely ignore her. This time, *she* ignored him.

Who would have thought this was how she would be spending her fall? Fleeing across the country to a supposedly desert safe-haven. Instead of enjoying the changing foliage colors in Michigan and Wisconsin—maybe lying on a Lake Michigan beach in the waning days of sun, or boating on Lake Geneva.

They had promised Father *all* were continuing to track the supposedly hired killer. *They* being the FBI, Illinois State Police, and various county Sheriff's departments across the country. "Not to worry," *they* had assured her father. Indeed, she had heard a snatched whisper at one of *their* meetings when "The Noiseless Killer" was mentioned as the hired-gun's name, and had to cover her mouth tightly to keep from laughing at such a silly name—*and* consequently being caught eavesdropping. *Noiseless? Now really.*

To *their* credit, Adeleine admitted, she did see the bulletins they sent out to law enforcement across the country. Then further, distributed on their networks everywhere— to hear *them* tell it. Though the bulletins were picture-less, since they didn't yet know exactly what the contract-killer looked like—just that one had been hired and his name. Informant information, her father had speculated.

Before getting her out of harm's way—her father eventually confided under her relentless questioning—there was a friend who was going to help. And that was where they were headed. Finally, around Kingman, Arizona, Winston revealed who his friend was. Judge Leigh-Everett Rhodes. And Judge Rhodes did not know they were coming.

A comforting revelation in some respects—but quite perplexing. It wasn't clear to her just how Judge Rhodes would or could help, even though she pushed the question with her father several times before actually arriving where they now were—going up his driveway in the Mojave.

And how the heck did Judge Rhodes end up out here? And why? Adeleine did guess at the reason why her father had picked him—and here. *The remoteness.* Who would possibly come looking for her out here in this strange place?

Her remembrance of Rhodes was that of a handsome man, *for his age,* a straight-shooter, and clearly intelligent. But most importantly, she thought, fair and not self-aggrandizing. Indeed, even rather reticent when it came to talking about himself and his accomplishments. She didn't consider him famous, but fairly well known in Illinois political circles. She had liked him.

Indeed, during the time she knew him, to her still youthful-eyes and sensibilities, he had "looked good" in court. Not just physically, but also his mannerisms. And invariably at trial's end, she thought his rulings were sound. Her father said Rhodes was well respected, and Adeleine never doubted he was. *But now this?*

Her thoughts switched from the man to his current environment. Her surroundings certainly did not fit the *California* she often saw in TV shows. Somewhere after Needles, and after making the last turn off I-40 heading toward their "hideout," Malcolm had informed them in a learned tone from his "front of the limo" world—they were in the "The Mojave Desert." Then he added in an even more all-knowing tone, "The nowadays interstate version of Route 66 if you want to get swiftly from town to town. Site to site."

Adeleine had caught sight of a small sign for a campground not far after their turning off the interstate. "Dad's RV Park" was it? And a little farther on, an even smaller sign with an arrow saying, "Shiné." Admittedly Route 66 was on her "want to do list," but again, *in a limousine* at seventy-miles an hour on interstate highways was not how she had imagined "doing the road."

However, right now, and even with the sacrilege of having traveled for about nineteen-hundred plus miles so far of Route 66 without really stopping anywhere, Adeleine straightened her shoulders, then wiggled her butt a bit—bringing her thin and rather short sitting-stature to full height. Though not a tall person, she found herself often combating a tendency to slump; whether standing at her full five-feet-four, or sitting as she was now.

She guessed the back of a limousine was probably more comfortable than on the back of a Hog. Or, in a two-seater. Or even in a Corvette for that matter. The limo experience, however, was not quite the same. She smiled slightly.

After adjusting her posture, Adeleine also reminded her emotions, *I promised father I'd do this*. For sure, she would never forget his pleading eyes that day in Illinois—almost on the verge of tears—not a common emotion for him. It was quite clear to her at that moment, his usual bravado and omnipresent political demeanor were not in the forefront. He was seriously rattled by something or someone. For sure, her heart had swelled with love that moment. *My father.* For better or worse. And her emotions swelled again now in the remembering. She almost reached across her armrest to grab his hand; but on second thought, refrained. Instead, she smiled to herself, then turned her head to the driveway scenery out her window, remembering the rest of those moments. *Not many days ago.*

They were talking, eye to eye in their Illinois home's ostentatious faux-manor-house library—the rows and rows of perfectly matching book spines were still vivid in her mind. He was holding the latest threatening letter in shaking hands. Again, very much out of character for Winston Moore.

"You need to get out of harm's way. Fast," he'd murmured that awful morning—his voice low in volume, but with frightening intensity. Even now, she involuntary shuddered from remembered fear. And at the time, she perceived his emotions as genuine. *Not a made up event like some he's perpetrated in the past.*

So many times she had just wanted to get away from Illinois. Get away from her father's power-and-influence umbrella. *As life sometimes is,* she now further reflected, *there's a bizarre irony lacing this whole thing.* For thinking then, and now still, *I need my own life.* A life based upon her alone. *My accomplishments, not my father's.* Though her friend in Peoria, Betty, occasionally scolded her, "You're soooooo lucky. Your path to success laid out before you. No struggles, no hassles. Wish your dad was my dad."

But now, the reality of having actually left Illinois, *a fait accompli,* and with Malcolm driving up the final stretch of a driveway she would never imagined existed—Adeleine was having a hard time assimilating the world materializing around them, and connecting the dots between her past desires and her current reality. A forest-green colored tree-lined drive, a stone circular driveway, several teak benches, thick green hedges—and the house...*a castle? And in the middle of the desert?*

Giving up, her mind boggled and she stopped trying to understand. *Alice in wonderland,* for this was neither a place she personally could have imagined, nor a world she could visualize Judge Leigh-Everett Rhodes living in. *No,* it was definitely like being a stranger in an alien land. Eerily, the car-buffeting winds had disappeared. No blowing sand or debris. And complete silence. *Unnerving,* she thought.

She heard the intercom click on, then all-knowing Malcolm informed them, "Winds are not as bad right here, and no sand. It's all the trees. We're here at the house. I'll go to the door."

And some doors they were. Massive, with insets from top to bottom with double stained glass.

"Holy Hannah," Adeleine heard herself say aloud.

Funny, Chief of Police Glover Deers thought while making himself "take a moment." A conscious focusing habit he retained from years back. He needed to pull back, and look around. *Mentally deep breathe.* Understand if he could, what the heck was going on.

It could have been hard to concentrate, given all the dust and dirt flying around on I-40—but for some reason, Glover found the freeway hum part calming. Odd how when the traffic noise was just right, seemingly droning through an otherwise silent background—it was like a highway-styled whistling of the trees on a crisp fall morning. Though, he mused, one could hardly compare the combined decibels of thousands of internal combustion engines to mother nature's whistling trees. Or could he? Indeed, he could still remember the "sound of the city" from his metro days.

Still, it is funny, though, he mentally reiterated—how he was these days finding the dust, dirt, and basic scrub desert scenery surrounding him comfortable. *I hated it when I first came here.* Yet now, in late morning brightness, and despite the grim crime-scene situation he was in the middle of, Glover was no longer uncomfortable in the Mojave. His mother Margaret had told him on several occasions, "In some ways, the desert will steal your soul." She was right. *As usual.*

"I wonder," he murmured to himself as he straightened his back and pulled himself to full height outside his Crown Victoria cruiser. He still needed, though, to steady his quite solidly built frame against his passenger door from the wind's power. In his current observing position, he could also keep an eye on his Mobile Data Terminal inside his cruiser. Glover had his cell and radio with him, but his MDT could transmit so much information these days. And quickly.

Suddenly, in a matter of a few seconds, the I-40 medium strip became completely calm. No longer any gusts, nor flying dust particles. He wondered, *eye of the storm passing over?*

Ben Bellaeu had let Glover know he already called Forensics in Needles before heading to the Cajon Pass pile up which Ben also said was blocked, and San Bernardino deputies and CHP "down below" were probably non-starters when it came to help. *There's always CHP and SBC aviation support,* Glover now reflected. He smiled vaguely and clicked out the side of his mouth. He considered Ben Bellaeu a funny sort of guy, and figured there were multiple reasons why he'd wanted to get away from this dead body and dump the problem on him.

Ending his "taking a moment," and under protection of the "eye-of-the-storm," Glover walked back to the culvert, making sure his "Smokey the Bear" hat—*as Leiv called it*—was securely attached to his head—even though calmness still prevailed. *Don't trust these darned Mojave winds one bit.* He glanced down at his feet, and at the moment there weren't even any dust-devils swirling around as he walked.

Ahead of him near the culvert, the Needles Coroner's team was also on scene and had taken over the area. Glover noticed Deputy Sheriffs Brad Temper and Tanya Lewis had yet to arrive—but he knew they were only moments away. His smile lingered a bit, figuring both deputies would be pleased at this momentary calm. This stretch along I-40 was not prized for pleasant desert weather.

Traffic was not heavy, and moving in a rather controlled flow going east—because of the Cajon Pass mess he figured. There was also the presence of his cruiser and the coroner's van psychologically slowing traffic in both directions.

Not much more I can do here, Glover thought as he considered logistics and what next. For sure, he did want another look at that culvert now the body was removed and loaded. *Ready for transport.* But before actually forcing himself to look for a second time into the dirty darkness of that manmade cave, he procrastinated by deciding his next few steps. When Brad and Tanya arrived, he would ask them to follow him back to the office. There was a new flyer he'd just received and put up from back east somewhere that he wanted them to look at.

In addition, there was something about this body in a culvert—bizarre, but at the same time, having a planned feel to it? But he couldn't yet figure out why. *A feel to it?* Glover almost laughed aloud at himself. As if a dead body in a culvert could have a "feel" to it—except sad.

But before heading to Shiné after they assessed the scene, Glover decided to invite the deputies to breakfast at the Ludlow Café. *Not far away.* Indeed, he had missed his French toast with Leiv, and he could feel and hear his stomach start to object at such flagrant mistreatment. *Leiv's probably still mad at me.* Might still be sitting there? He knew Leiv and Chef Jack were simpatico and could chew-the-fat a bit.

Glover's latest thought about Leiv and the chef caused his stomach to growl again.

"You mean the man on the ground came back to life?" Adeleine's eyes were bright and incredulous—reviving for Leiv a long-gone memory of her younger self sitting in his courtroom watching various court proceedings. Quickly, he dismissed the memory. *Silly nostalgia from another life. Another time.*

Reconnecting to the present, he leaned forward across Rhodes Castle's large kitchen table—*Hester's table*—and said directly to Adeleine sitting across from him, "Yes, it was the most amazing thing." Leiv almost added, *That I've ever seen.* But after his years on the bench, and his subsequent and unexpected Shiné adventures, he'd seen a lot. "It was the CPR," he added, remembering Walker Johns pounding on Lucca's chest. *More like Walker's determination.*

"Some would say a miracle," she murmured thoughtfully. "I knew something horrible had happened when we turned up your driveway. A fire you say?"

"Yes. Lucca Fabero is the caretaker for several pieces of land...looks like his doublewide caught on fire."

"An accident?"

First thing I wondered. He shrugged. "Probably, but don't know anything yet." He certainly would be talking to Walker as soon as he could.

Winston, sitting right next to him, cleared his throat in a loud and officious way that Leiv immediately remembered. *Some people never change.* Leiv said, "Terrible host, I am. Can I get the three of you something to drink? You must be hot and tired." He made sure to look up and over to the already introduced with one-name-only chauffeur, Malcolm—standing stiffly by the door between the carriage house and kitchen. "Especially you, Malcolm. After all that driving."

Malcolm smiled, and gave Leiv an ever-so-slight eye movement that Leiv fancied was a wink. "The use of your facilities would be well appreciated," Malcolm said in a formal employee tone of voice.

Leiv smiled in return. "The closest bathroom is right down this hall." He got up, and continuing to ignore Winston, made a motion for Malcolm to follow him, while also speaking the words, "Follow me, I'll show you."

It didn't take them long to arrive at the small guest bathroom halfway between the kitchen and the double-door front entry to Rhodes Castle. At the bathroom, before heading back, Leiv asked, "Is Winston flying back?"

Malcolm's expression turned wry and he looked quite directly and knowingly into Leiv's eyes. "No, I'm driving him back." Then evidently taking in Leiv's quizzical look, "I've been an employee of Mr. Moore five years now in various capacities. Has his ways, but in this I think he's right. They'll be monitoring the airports, looking for him." Then with a nod, Malcolm turned away and disappeared into the bathroom.

The minute Leiv opened the kitchen door, he heard Winston clear his throat again—as if he'd missed his censure the first time. Then Leiv caught himself midway in a reflex stepping action—looking to the floor right in front of the doorway to make sure he didn't step on Dobie. She was of course now in Hester and David's care. He sorely missed Dobie, but wasn't yet sure about his feelings on the absence of Hester. She had been such a "fixture" in his new Rhodes Castle life. *Wedding in just a week.* A thought which caused Leiv to smile, despite Winston's annoying behavior. Pleasant thoughts about Dobie, Hester, and David's new life together were a good counterbalance to the unexpected dropping of Winston Moore back into his life.

Clearly not wanting to afford Leiv another opportunity to ignore him, Winston declared without further waiting, "It's not quite a miracle I'm asking of you, Leigh-Everett..." He glanced at his daughter with a don't-interrupt-me-look. "But comes close to one." Then he smiled the smile of the masterful political-charmer Leiv had known before his Shiné sojourn.

Something big was going on with Winston, and it was quite clear he was about to be pulled into whatever it was—and Leiv wasn't sure he could do anything to stop whatever was coming. Or help if he could. *And it had all started so suddenly.*

Indeed, not much earlier, after watching Lucca leave for the hospital in a siren-wailing ambulance, and exchanging a few hasty words with the dumbstruck onlookers he knew—Leiv had forced himself away from the catastrophe across from his home, crossed over the road, and headed up LC's winding driveway. He figured somewhere in front of his house, a limousine awaited.

In several minutes he was home and pulling up to park in front of LC's carriage-house-styled garage where he usually parked his pickup. From there, Leiv saw a man and a woman sitting on the teak English garden bench to the side of LC's massive stained-glass double entry doors—only about a hundred or so feet away.

The two were hidden by Athols if viewed face on, but from his garage door perspective, LC and Everett's secret bench could be clearly seen. *The very same bench Charlie White and I chatted on,* Leiv mused and then murmured, "Must be something special about my bench." With those words, Leiv claimed the "bench" as his. *Neither Father's, nor LC's any longer.* Odd as the emotional connections were—he'd so much admired Charlie and the aerial photography work he did—and somehow that admiration helped him emotionally set his own feet quite firmly earthbound in Shiné on Rhodes Castle land.

Just this last spring.

In addition this morning, facing and parallel to the castle's front door, another man, in a chauffeur's uniform and cap no less, stood formally and slightly wide-legged next to the driver-side door of a black limousine.

This limo was modest, compared to some of the stretched ones he'd seen on I-15 headed from Los Angeles to Las Vegas—but a limo nonetheless. And looking quite out of place in the front driveway of Rhodes Castle. *A misplaced limousine*, he thought bemusedly.

All three people had looked his way. Clearly waiting for him. Unfortunately, triggered by the chauffeur's uniform, for a micro-second Leiv needed to fight back a flash of memory from Chicago again. *Melissa, the Congress Expressway, the back of a chauffeurs head, that horrible crash....*

But now, back in the present, with them all gathered in Hester's kitchen—*and his liking the situation or not*—it was time to give Winston Moore the floor. Stalling time was over. A tactic Leiv was aware he had been childishly employing since the moment he recognized the man sitting on his special bench.

Leiv was indeed very curious about what was going on, but a little devil in him had directed his side-stepping actions up to this moment. *Now,* it was time to grow up. Forget the past—*let bygones be bygones, as the saying goes.*

He noticed Adeleine had found some cold water bottles in the fridge while he and Malcolm were gone, and was now bringing them over. Leiv smiled her way, glad she was playing hostess for a bit in a new and strange environment. *An adaptable young woman,* he thought. He sat back down and consciously directed all his attention to Winston—plastering a courteous, even welcoming expression on his face.

Then taking in his sometimes mentor-of-sorts from Illinois directly, what he thought he saw in Winston's eyes, was unclear. *So long ago since we've interacted.* Was it the look of a man searching for a position of strength from which to reassert himself? *No,* Leiv decided on further thought, *for once, it's that he's a stranger in a very strange land. Uncertain?*

Winston's facial expression and body language indicated he was searching for a touchstone to anchor himself. *Help him understand where the heck he was, and what the heck his former rising-star Judge Leigh-Everett Rhodes was doing here?* Of course, Leiv added to his assessment—*Winston must know something about my living situation, my current life choices. Otherwise, why would he drive out here?*

Winston was evidently counter-guessing at Leiv's thoughts and manner. "Nice here, even though not at all what I expected." He smiled from behind an expression of dumbfoundedness. "There's no civilization around. No other houses or businesses. Maybe in that town further down the road?" Winston turned in his chair to lean in toward Leiv and cocked his head. "But I can see how that situation could have its advantages."

The man still has his politician's savvy. He's managed to combine incredulity, condescension, and empathy effortlessly. Leiv remembered quite well, in the old days some of Winston's critics—unkindly Leiv now reflected—had summed him up as being only intellectually passable by their standards, while acting in tone and mannerisms like he was intellectually superior. "Half smart," followed by one of several alliterative like-sounding and profane pejoratives, were the descriptions Leiv most remembered being used behind Winston's back.

That aspect of Winston's personality hadn't much bothered Leiv—having seen so many similar attributes in the lawyers he was always dealing with. *Defense and prosecuting.* Funny though, their intellectual superiority posturing was seldom effective, *juries saw right through it.* Remembering, Leiv held back a smile at seeing again those juror-looks of incredulity. *The past. And a different life.* Quickly, Leiv brought his mind back to current day Winston Moore.

"No Art Institute, or major colleges?" Winston's tone was now more condescending, even accusing.

Leiv tried to hold back on calling him on his attitude, but was unable to stop an instant knee-jerk reaction to defend his new Shiné home. "We're only a couple hours from Vegas or LA. There's "stuff" there to match whatever you come up with in Illinois." Leiv felt childish once his words were out. Still, he spread his hands in a "what do you say to that" gesture, and smiled smugly.

"Anything matching the University of Illinois or University of Chicago or Loyola or DePaul...?" Winston was clearly willing to give equally childish tit-for-tat shots, then shook his head and took a long swallow of cold water from the bottle Adeleine handed him.

Leiv started mentally compiling a list of schools— University of Nevada, ArtCenter College of Design, Stanford, various University of California campuses, Loyola Marymount— but midstream, maturity caught up with him and he decided to give the round to Winston—almost shaking his head in dismay at his own childishness. *Winston still knows how to push my buttons. So why bring your daughter here?*

Instead, in what he hoped was an accommodating host tone, Leiv asked, "Do you think Malcolm is okay?" Actually, he figured Malcolm had preferred to take his leave out the front— seeking quiet, maybe a nap even—in the comfort of his limo. *Without* his trip companions.

Winston Moore, also a retired judge, a former politician, and still an Illinois big-wig, shook his head dismissively, his face saying he barely gave Leiv's question any thought.

Adeleine said, "Father, Malcolm might need some water, or maybe a nap?"

Winston turned to her—and to give him his due—from his facial expression it looked to Leiv like his daughter's thoughts and words were actually important to him.

"You know," she continued, "It's been a very long trip."

He smiled at her. "Of course, dear. And before he and I leave, I'll make sure he's okay in all respects."

An act? Leiv wasn't sure. *Or real consideration based on love?*

Looking back at Leiv, Winston returned to their conversation. "Is there a bar even? In this town of yours?" This time there was the hint of a twinkle in Winston's eye. "And farms, cornfields?"

Leiv laughed outright. Couldn't help it. Amazingly, he noted, Winston was also now smiling. "There's alfalfa farms farther east of here. In Newton. And yes, there is a bar at TGS."

"TGS?"

"The Greasy Spoon. Restaurant and bar down the road in Shiné."

Winston shook his head and allowed an expression of dismay to spread across his face. "What a fool I'm being." Then he smiled. A smile that almost looked self-deprecating.

Leiv was amazed. In fifteen-plus years of knowing this man back in Illinois, he couldn't remember Winston ever admitting to anything close to being foolish or wrong. He hoped his own incredulity was not flashing brightly across his forehead.

In fact, in the past when he and Winston's lives were intertwined, the few smiles he witnessed on Winston's long and angular face had seemed more like grimaces. Like it pained him to smile. In remembering, Leiv was also surprised at his current ambivalent opinion of Winston. *A difficult man to like or hate.*

"I need your help." Winston held up his hand, indicating he wanted him to wait—have patience to hear him out. "And the reason I came here to Shiner, is because Shiner—"

Leiv nonetheless did interrupt, "Shiné."

"Shiné," Winston corrected without complaint, "...is because there's nothing here. No direct flights, no places to hideout and ambush." His voice caught for a second.

Another occurrence Leiv had never seen in Winston's constellation of personality traits.

A few moments passed, as if a time was needed for logical thought to catch up with emotions. *For both of us,* Leiv thought. He looked to Adeleine. She was looking down at her hands clutching her water bottle—also being held in their moments of pause.

Then in his characteristic way of changing the subject and coming in sideways, Winston returned Leiv to current-moment realities. "You're different now." Winston turned his head in a dramatic manner. "Yes, you've changed quite a bit you know."

This time, the look on Winston's face was so contrived and reeking of affectation, Leiv had to force himself to remain objective. "It's been a few years." He was pleased at the flatness he heard in his own voice. *And, I guess Winston is actually right. I have changed.*

"I want to leave my daughter here with you." Winston sighed heavily, then turned his head to look out Hester's kitchen window—where unbeknownst to him, Hester had for many years tended her rose and vegetable gardens. "They're trying to kill us. And I just won't have it."

Cajon Pass was a nightmare. Not so much because "what to do" was difficult for CHP Officer Ben Bellaeu, but the repetition—over, and over, and over—giving the same information out to drivers wore on him.

Once in "Cajon Pass" proper, driver options were extremely limited. Sit, wait, and fume until one could move forward—or turn around and go back on the two lanes heading back on each side designated for that purpose. Ben Bellaeu's job was to monitor the northeast bound lanes, giving a standard spiel to northeastern-bound drivers who'd endured stop-and-go inching forward movement through the pass. They needed to know that ahead was also slow going until around Barstow, where traffic could then split between I-40 and I-15.

Most drivers and passengers were tired and overwhelmed by their situation. Dour usually, some downright hostile. *And who wouldn't be?* Especially if you were heading to a job—and faced with three hours to complete a journey through the Cajon Pass that usually took ten minutes. Or worse, having to go back to where they'd just left. *All because an idiot in a pricey Mercedes sports car pushed it too far. Red of course.*

While occupied with his red-car bias, a white rental car— Ben could tell "rental" from the window sticker—was next in line, and the man inside was smiling with what Ben recognized as a hapless-tourist expression. *But something about his expression.*

"Good morning, Officer."

Ben gave the man his "what to expect ahead" little speech, then waved him on. It wasn't until the driver and car were slowly moving away that Ben felt that itchy feeling run down his back. An instinctual itch he never neglected to scratch. *Something for sure.*

Quickly, he memorized the license plate number to check when back in his cruiser and had a couple spare minutes. Even rentals could be checked in California law enforcement databases.

Yep, *something*—and Ben was going to find out what.

It had been the longest of days for Adeleine. The hours from when their limo first turned off the road marked with the little sign to Shiné and then heading up that curved driveway and encountering Rhodes Castle for the first time—seemed interminable.

Then seeing Judge Rhodes after so many years....

So much to take in. Especially now that she was alone in this strange place. Her father and Malcolm declined Judge Rhodes's offer of at least overnight hospitality, and started their trip home almost immediately. She was officially "dropped off." *More like dumped.*

Adeleine was confused and scared. She hadn't really understood the full extent of the death threats against her father, and against her by extension, until this very afternoon when Winston laid it all out for Judge Rhodes. *Whom I'm supposed to start calling Leiv.*

And as if that wasn't enough to take in, she was now having a wrap up *tete-a-tete*—in this large and state-of-the-art kitchen—with a woman who had entered the kitchen unannounced through the garage-cum-carriage house door. A woman dressed in the most colorful combination of blouse and skirt she'd ever seen. Her name was Hester Miller. *And* she was Leiv's former housekeeper. *And* was getting married next Sunday. Right here at this strange place called Rhodes Castle.

New and unimagined events were coming at Adeleine with a rapidity she could barely keep up with. There was also a sweet-eyed Doberman this woman had brought with her now stretched across the threshold into the kitchen from the hallway. "Dobie," she was told.

"I still have a few last things to pick up, you see," Hester was saying while eyeing Adeleine intently. "Don't want to come back after we're married."

Is she now giving me the evil-eye? Adeleine mused kindly in that Hester had already spent considerable time explaining her Miller-Gypsy-heritage and "powers." This unique woman also had touched cryptically on fake Mojave-Stones with a disgusted look and shake of the head. Adeleine hadn't really understood, or pushed her for details. Just listened.

They progressed to drinking what Adeleine thought was the worst tasting tea she'd ever forced down, and consequently only drank half a sip at the most, while making a big to-do over its uniqueness. The leaves were produced from a tin on a high-up cupboard shelf and brewed by Hester in a bright-purple tea pot— produced from another high-up cupboard. There were several tins marked "tea" where this one came from and Adeleine wondered if they might taste better? Maybe she'd try one later.

"And I can read minds," Hester continued, but now with a wry smile and a change in her eyes to a decided twinkle.

What a complicated woman, Adeleine thought in response.

"Yes I am," Hester said, agreeing with her thought.

Adeleine felt her jaw drop, then started laughing. In a second Hester joined in.

"I like you," Adeleine said after their simpatico laugh. "Mind reading and all. But this tea is awful."

"You just wait and see how you feel later. Drink it all after I leave. My tea will do wonders to relax you. The others on the shelf, too."

How does she know I need to relax?

Hester smiled knowingly and changed the topic. "It's Saturday night gathering time tonight. David and I will be here, so I want to make my special Gypsy punch to bring."

Adeleine smiled and nodded.

"David likes Leigh-Everett," Hester added in a tone that sounded to Adeleine like justification for something?

Hester had insisted first thing on a house-proud kind of tour of LC's grand castle, and Adeleine, of course hadn't objected. Not only did she want to know who this woman was, but fill in any bits of the judge's history since Illinois. And of course, see this strange castle-house.

She had listened during their tour to bits here and there, in various rooms, about Hester Miller's mother, Hester Miller Senior, and her influence on making the place what it was today. It was a pleasant walk around—second floor and first, even outside a bit. All the while Dobie accompanied them. Clearly, the canine was quite fond of Hester.

Bits and pieces. She would need time later to put together Hester's haphazard historical tidbits.

There were several "things" however, Adeleine did pick up on right off, and wanted to ask Judge Rhodes—*Leiv*—about. The library for instance. Hester seemed reluctant to enter, and once inside acted quite unsure. Adeleine also wanted to see what Hester called the "bird perch," but she didn't take her up to. A glassed in room atop the structure—a room she hadn't noticed while they waited for Leiv to come home and find them.

After they returned to the kitchen, and uncannily on cue with Adeleine's thoughts, Leiv entered, smiled broadly on seeing Dobie stretched across the threshold, then squatted to pet the Doberman fondly on the head and behind her ears. The dog's nubby tail thumping on the floor told Adeleine there was mutual fondness there. *Another backstory?*

Hester stood on Leiv's arrival and brushed the front of her multi-colored long crinkly skirt with her hands as if drying them. "Leigh-Everett," Hester said, quickly acknowledging Leiv's presence. "I've come back to pick up some ingredients for tonight."

Adeleine watched as Leiv stood for several moments, with a rather childlike and dumbfounded expression on his face; as if he were in a cartoon skit, starting with a squinting of his eyes, then rubbing his forehead as if trying to remember something. Not an expression Adeleine expected to ever see on Judge Leigh-Everett-Rhodes's face.

To her relief—perceiving this as maybe an awkward moment for reasons unknown to her—the judge finally smiled broadly. It was a smile she *did* recognize from long gone days. An easy smile, likable and accommodating. "Hester. Great seeing you. I'm looking stupid because I completely forgot it was Saturday night already." He shook his head. "Glad you remembered, and even gladder you're coming tonight. Right?"

Hester raised her chin and looked directly at Leiv, "David said I should."

"Great. I need to prepare myself—"

Before he could finish, Hester took steps toward the carriage house door and said, "Got to get back to our trailer and get ready."

Adeleine held back her own questions as she and Leiv stood on opposite sides of the table—both watching Hester leave with Dobie trotting happily behind. She instinctively knew a lot was being said—or not said—in the exchange between Hester Miller and her former boss. Unfortunately—after her long journey and "dumped" status here in the middle of the desert, right in the middle of other people's lives, events, and emotions—her tiredness was increasing and her patience waning.

Evidently her feelings were being reflected on her face— or the Judge, Leigh-Everett, *Leiv*, was also a mind reader.

He said, "You want a shot of something? Harvey's Bristol Crème, or B&B, or a glass of Bordeaux, or a beer?" He blew out a puff of air. "I shouldn't have left you alone for so long. But I needed to try to reach Chief Deers...." He let his sentence drift to nothing.

She felt her shoulders relax, and laughed. "Do I look that stressed?"

He nodded. "When I left earlier you looked like you were barely handling all this." He made a sweeping motion with his arms. "But meeting Hester has thrown even more 'stuff' your way. I didn't know she was coming by. I wonder if David dropped her off...or she walked...I was outside on my cell and I didn't see him pull up."

"You know," Adeleine interrupted mischievously, and with a smile. "Your castle could do with a bit of a cleaning."

"Hester's appraisal?" He smiled in return. "And I was on the phone long enough for you to take a tour?"

"She took me on a quick tour looking for you. We didn't know where you were. I thought you were in the hall or upstairs. And she did mention offhandedly, 'things were going down the toilet,' since she left." Adeleine pulled out a chair, and with body-language indicated her desire for him to take a few moments to talk some more.

An unexpected look appeared on his face. *Embarrassment?* Couldn't be over housekeeping stuff—she doubted he was a stickler in that area. But he took her meaning, sat, and looked at her quite directly—as if saying, *"you have my full attention."*

Adeleine wasn't sure why, but words just started bubbling out. "You know, they promised us the FBI and County Sheriff's departments were tracking the Noiseless Killer—"

"Noiseless Killer?"

"Beats me where that silly name came from." She rubbed her hand along the edge of the well-polished kitchen table. And contrary to Hester's spin, it felt spotless. She guessed the wood was oak, yet the grain was pronounced enough for her to feel, and the stain was dark. She hadn't really noticed earlier. Then she shrugged. "I was only around Father and an agent once, but I'm pretty sure that agent said 'noiseless.' And he assured us, 'We have bulletins everywhere. All the way across the country.'"

Looking up from the lovely table and back at Leiv, she realized he was not only looking intently into her eyes, but also giving the impression he was assessing her entire face. *Maybe seeing Father in my wide-set eyes and broad mouth?*—a thought which led her down a memory tangent she proceeded to verbalize. "I remember several nights in Father's study—with Father and his friends like you. Listening." She felt her cheeks warming—and wondered why. "Once discussing the balancing act required between the law and what was right." Adeleine had indeed forgotten the good friendship and times back then.

I was so young. And quite suddenly, Adeleine realized on an emotional level why she was here. *Oh yes,* despite all the other things her father was, he would do his best to protect his little girl. And where else to bring her—but here? To an old friend he could trust.

"I remember those times..." Leiv muttered. She noticed he averted his eyes—ever so quickly. "...I was just thinking," he continued to look down for a few seconds before adding, "how you look a lot like him."

I'm right. He was assessing her looks. Adeleine started to laugh—then caught herself. Retaining her composure but letting a wry smile curl the corners of her mouth, she said, "I know you meant it as a compliment. But saying I look like a man—even if it is my father, is a dubious compliment at best.

They both laughed—comfortably, Adeleine thought. *I think I'll weather this new situation. With Judge Rhodes's help.* Still thoughtful, she continued in their Winston vein, "Father is still a smart-aleck with a very occasional whimsical bend, but I'm afraid since he stopped being a judge..." She paused, searching for the right way to express herself. "...since he jumped into the political arena his 'speak' has became more and more political in tone." After a breath, she added, "And I guess his actions, too."

"And I'm thinking politics is at the basis of your flight across the country?"

"I believe he didn't do a favor for someone he promised he would." She looked out the window toward what Hester said had been her garden. "Conscience got to him before it was too late." She looked down at her hands, and an aberrant unconnected thought popped into her consciousness. *Wonder if I have a green thumb?* Truth was, even in the agricultural lushness of Illinois, she'd never tried growing anything.

"Do you know the details?"

She shook her head. "Father refused to tell me what started all of this." *Trying to protect me.*

"Probably trying to protect you."

She looked up, and again he was staring at her. And it didn't feel bad.

Changing the subject a bit, he asked, "So what are you doing these days?"

She really didn't want to talk about herself—while at the same time wanting him to know her a little better. "Well, you know I wanted to be a lawyer. Trial—like dad was. Then a judge.

And then eventually, my ultimate pie-in-the-sky dream, a supreme court justice." Adeleine heard herself make a deprecating little sound. "You know, the grand dreams of youth."

Leiv's face told her that he did know.

"I went to quite a few of Dad's court cases, when they'd let me." She didn't mention the hours spent sitting in Leiv's courtroom. "I even pulled the 'nepotism' string a couple times to get in on several of the sensational ones."

She sighed, and thought, *how easy to talk to this man.* "Wanting to feel the *reality*, you know, of *real* crimes. *Real* victims." Adeleine looked away for a few seconds—this time towards the carriage house door Hester and Dobie had entered from, and hurried out of.

When she returned her attention to Leiv, she looked at him straight on, knowing she was conveying a little pleading for understanding in her eyes. Hoping he knew what she was trying to articulate. "It was the victims I felt the most sorry for. Most of the time, I was on their side." She held up her hand in a "wait" gesture and felt her face warm. "It was a common saying, '*The Law* is the law—*Justice* is another thing."

"I remember," Leiv smiled. "And you've brought up several mental conundrums of my earlier days." He returned his eyes to hers. "And you're a justice kind of gal?"

Adeleine laughed outright, feeling relaxed at last. "You know, Judge, the word 'gal' isn't exactly in favor these days."

The Chief and the two San Bernardino County deputies ended up eating breakfast in Glover Deer's Shiné Police Office. The assistant Chef Jack left to tend TGS had prepared biscuit-type sandwiches, deep fried hash-brown patties, and pancakes—with one chocolate shake on the side.

Deputy Brad Temper had wanted to go to Dairy Queen in Ludlow so he could have a chocolate shake with his breakfast, Deputy Tanya Lewis wanted to have pancakes at The Ludlow Café, and Glover just wanted to eat. In the end, he had called Chef Jack in Shiné to ask if he would put to-go meals together for the three of them. He wasn't there—still at the fire aftermath he and Leiv had just talked about via cell phone. But his assistant chef, whose name Glover couldn't remember, took his order.

Good idea on my part—to come back here and eat first before jumping into anything else. Though on their way back to Shiné, in two cruisers, Glover and his tag-along Needles deputies did stop at Lucca's charred house remains long enough to find out Lucca was already on his way to Barstow hospital via I-15, and a fire investigation team was on their way to the scene from Vegas. Local Fire Chief Parnell also told them with few words—he didn't really want, or need him and two deputies tromping around "his" scene before they had everything sorted out. "I'll come to your office as soon as I can," he'd promised.

Ordinarily, Glover would have insisted on a briefing right then, but decided to back off. The Marshal was competent, covered a big area, and knew when and from whom he needed help.

He now took a second mouth-stretching bite out of his flakey biscuit—layered inside with a fried egg, bacon, cheddar cheese, and some special Chef Jack sauce that Glover couldn't begin to guess at the ingredients. *Delicious, whatever it is.* He was glad they were eating first before trying to strategize—and hopefully he wasn't dribbling the sauce down his chin and looking like an oaf.

Glover had even taken off his "Smokey the Bear" campaign hat and placed it carefully on the corner of his desk before starting to eat. The two deputies were wolfing-down their food on the other side of his office at the guest desk—so he figured his prized hat was safe enough. Who cared about sauce dribbling down his chin—but grease on his hat, *well that was another matter.*

Nonetheless, the cloud of knowing Lucca was injured and his house burned to the ground hung in his emotions. *I'll call the hospital after I eat, and see how he's doing.*

In the meantime, Glover figured he and the deputies could eat, think, and share their thoughts so far on the I-40 body. Indeed, he hoped that together—two San Bernardino County Deputies and one Shiné Chief of Police could decide what to jurisdictionally do about the body heading to the Needles coroner. *A body Ben Bellaeu had dropped on him.*

For the time being it was his problem—well, *our* combined problem at this point. But Glover would definitely like to change the "who's responsible" situation—and his current preference if he could, was to pass the whole thing back to CHP. If they wanted his local Shiné involvement, or the Sheriff Department's, then they could ask for it through official channels. Especially now with this fire situation in his piece of the Mojave.

A fire that certainly could be arson. *Nah,* who would want to kill Lucca?

But, his queasy gut earlier had not only complained to him about hunger, but also sent him a red-flag type warning at the fire scene. *But about what and who?* Glover wasn't yet sure.

There was for sure, however, something about this dead body in the culvert niggling at him. *Was there a tie to Shiné?* That didn't make any sense, nor could he imagine what the connection could possibly be. At the culvert, before the victim's body was bagged, Glover forced himself to look at the dead man's face straight on. Re-visualizing now, he didn't think he'd ever seen him before.

Yet, *maybe?* And could Lucca's home fire also be connected in some crazy-kind of way?

From across the space between desks, Deputy Brad Temper's expression and words mirrored Glover's thoughts. "You know, I looked at that guy's face real good again before the

EMTs zipped-him and took the body away." He'd already finished his breakfast and wiped his mouth. He then made a distasteful sound and a shiver-like gesture that Glover recognized the emotion behind. Dead bodies were never viewed easily—no matter how long in the force.

He cleaned up his own mess, got up, then went to sit with the deputies. The spare desk they were now all gathered around was one Glover maintained near the front of his storefront office for visiting law enforcement. Now taking their little group in, Glover observed they were a companionable working group.

Brad continued, "He wasn't in that bad of a shape given the circumstances." He rumpled up his paper towel placemat and used it to rub off his mouth and chin yet again before getting up, tossing the paper towel wad in the trash and walking over to the cork bulletin board in the "Break Room" area of the office. Affording only his back to their view.

Glover suspected Brad was not feeling as sanguine as he would like him and Tanya to think. Fairly seasoned for his time and age, but none the less, still a human being.

After a moment, and even though Brad's back was still turned to them, Glover sensed something new was up with Brad. *Something in the way he's holding himself....*

"Yes." Brad proclaimed loudly, now with full body emphasis and an arm movement recognizable even viewing him from the rear. "Here he is. Right here. Right under our G—" he caught himself and turned around to face him and Tanya at the table. "Right under our gosh-darn noses."

Glover laughed before he thought, then heard Tanya laughing with him. She said, "You don't have to clean up your language for me. Remember, I work in the same department you do. Heard it all."

Brad looked embarrassed, so Glover quickly moved things along. "Back to your comment—here who is?" He got up and walked over to Brad where the bulletin board hung. It was a big corkboard-type, which he himself kept up-to-date and looked

59

at, if only cursory, several times daily. He received many bulletins and pictures electronically, but Glover printed many out and tacked them up carefully on the board. *Luddite dinosaur.* But it was the way he still liked doing things, even with all the latest apps and gadgets. Besides, there was no one to please besides himself and the people of Shiné. He smiled at the phrase "the people of Shiné." *LC, Everett, and now Leiv's people.*

Glover was curious to see what Brad was seeing amongst all the items on his board. *Clearly I've missed something I put up here.* It only took a second after arriving at Brad's side for Glover's own recognition-sense to also kick in. The picture now jumped out at him—a rather big mug shot at that—showing a man, front and side, who very much indeed resembled the dead body in the culvert on I-40. Even with only seeing once, and now remembering the John Doe's work-site scarred face this morning, the resemblance was striking. "Sure could be him," Glover said and took a step closer and squinted. "The set of the chin...or is it the distance between the eyes—"

"It's a birthmark. Or is it a tattoo?" Brad stepped closer to the board also, and squinted like Glover. "See, Chief Deers?" He pointed to a mark at the base of the neck on the side view mug shot.

Glover leaned even closer and touched the picture. "You mean that piece of dirt?" He brushed at the spot, but nothing came off the picture.

"Where's the file for the photo?" Tanya asked from their rear. Glover turned to see she was now sitting at his desk, staring into his monitor. He smiled inwardly noticing she had moved his hat to atop his memo file cabinet. *Out of harms way.* But not having a clue right off as to what she was asking or how to respond, he needed a few seconds to get on board.

Before Glover could stumble into an answer, Brad quickly took the lead—heading over to Tanya, and proceeding to lean over her seated back. "The Chief doesn't go to The Criminal Justice Information System or the California Law Enforcement

Telecommunication System directly. If I remember correctly, click on that computer-shaped icon on the bottom right of the screen."

"This one?"

"Yes, takes you directly to the Cloud. Office 365."

Glover stopped listening to them exchange what he considered techno-babble. The San Bernardino County IT person had set him up, showed him what buttons to push to get bulletins and mug shots. Same with CHP. Enough knowledge for him.

Though Glover did figure he now knew the purpose for what they were doing, and turned back around and walked over to his floor model printer—a printer Leiv had insisted he purchase and personally paid for. The printer sat quite prominently not far from their break area. Glover waited. His expectation—a fresh bulletin would be appearing momentarily.

"Chief," Brad called to him, "She's printing another copy. We've upped the contrast and resolution to six-hundred. I'm thinking that's the max your printer will do?"

Unconsciously disregarding his cherished "luddite" status, Glover contributed, "It's actually twelve-hundred by six-hundred dpi. Leiv insisted."

"Great," Glover heard Tanya say behind him, and before he could turn to look at her in acknowledgement, his printer light started blinking, the motor started humming smoothly, and the top edge of what he suspected was a new mug shot, inched forward into the printout-bin section. From the first inch or so of picture as it progressed into view, Glover could see it was much sharper than the one he pinned up. *I'll have to find out what she did.* "Much better," he complimented loudly.

When Glover and the two San Bernardino deputies were jointly standing in front of his cork board, staring at the new and enhanced picture dubbed "The Noiseless Killer," he nodded and noticed in his peripheral vision, they were nodding in sync with him.

"Looks like we all agree." Without waiting for follow-on verbal responses, Glover charged ahead, getting what he thought were the necessary balls rolling. "I'll contact the coroner, make sure he checks for that birthmark."

Brad said, "I'll contact our office in Needles to see if there's any more info, or some contacts we might already have."

Tanya said, "There's a contact source back in Illinois on this. I'll give that office in Springfield a call directly...." She was simultaneously talking and walking toward the phone on the spare desk they were just eating on.

"Thank you Deputy Sheriff Lewis, and Deputy Sheriff Temper." Glover's mental-wheels were also rolling in another direction. With a moniker like The Noiseless Killer, their dead body was most probably a contract killer. A definite scumbag. *But I need to connect some more dots.*

Vaguely, he heard Brad say, "Chief Deers, we don't mind if you call us what we call each other."

"And what is that?" Glover asked, moving in tunnel-vision fashion toward his desk and top file drawer right below his hat. He heard their answer, mentally filed it away, but didn't really pay a lot of attention. No, he wanted to find a Las Vegas newspaper clipping from a few months back.

Once back sitting, and rummaging through his clippings-folder, he also heard Brad say, "We'll get on this right away. Times-a-flying and it's Saturday."

"Meaning?" Glover asked absently.

"Saturday night. You know, 'The Gathering.'"

Finally, he shifted his attention to the deputy. "Saturday night? The Gathering?" For a couple seconds, Glover felt a mild flash of anger. These two young deputies had successfully made him feel like a dullard several times in a very short period of time.

"Judge Rhodes? At his house. Drinking aperitifs and discussing issues."

The way Deputy Brad Temper reminded him it was Leiv's regular Saturday night get together caused Glover to look at him straight on. *Yes,* he was smiling. Teasingly, but definitely friendly-like. Glover's momentary flash of anger quickly vanished, and Glover joined in on Brad's tease himself. "So they call it 'The Gathering,' now?"

The deputy nodded. "That's what I've heard here in town. Like from the antiques lady, and TGS's cook, and Doc."

Glover smiled. "You know, I only started going a little while ago. That's probably when they started calling it 'The Gathering.'"

They both laughed. Glover didn't like cliques and "in-groups" and found it ludicrous to classify Leiv's withdrawing room get together as such. In fact, he mused, *I wonder what LC would think.* What he knew of his grandfather led him to think he would be laughing his head off. *Or, maybe pleased?*

Then it clicked what Deputy Brad Temper had said a moment earlier about his and Deputy Tanya Lewis's salutation convention. "Did you say you call each other Deputy Tanya— and Deputy Brad?"

Brad nodded, and Tanya smiled at him from the visitor-desk where she was still standing.

Glover clamped his teeth together and tightened his jaw muscles to keep from bursting out laughing.

Leiv will love this when I tell him.

Chapter Three
Assessing Positions

From LC's journal: Sometimes it's really hard a figuring out what's important and what ain't. Viola is good at it. Me, only middling.

Saturday Night: LC's Withdrawing Room

"These glasses are quite nice. I don't think you've brought them out before." Pastor Apply placed his just-drained aperitif glass down next to the almost empty Harvey's Bristol Crème bottle sitting on the nested Edwardian table in its customary spot between their well-padded and well-worn armchairs. All was as it should be for Leiv's Saturday night "gathering" in LC's cherished withdrawing room.

Leiv laughed lightly. "I didn't 'bring them out' before, Lloyd, because I didn't know they existed." He shifted his weight a little so he could turn sideways and see the look of appreciation on his friend's face his voice had implied. "Adeleine found a box on a lower back shelf this afternoon. I think she was looking for something to put in those little quiche kind of things we both just ate a bunch of."

Lloyd smiled at Adeleine and made a modest *bon appétit* hand gesture accompanied by a low-keyed foodie smack of his lips. Returning to the glasses, the Pastor retrieved his delicate-looking and slender little glass, this time holding it up at a postured viewing angle—squinting his eyes and reappraising. "They're very nice, antique do you think?"

"Don't know. There was an old label on the back saying something like…" Leiv turned back straight in his chair, closed his eyes, and let his head sink backwards into the plushy head padding of his armchair. "I think there were words something like Moser—hand blown—Lady Hamilton—gem color—etched— gold banded, I think."

From the pastor's left on the loveseat next to Margaret Deers, Adeleine said, "That's exactly what the label read. I'm surprised you remembered so well." She looked apologetically to Margaret next to her, and then to Lloyd, and finally to Leiv. "Sorry, guess I was eavesdropping. I thought they were quite pretty, too." She made a modest gesture with her hands, and added, "Fits the room, I thought." Then to Leiv's surprise, Adeleine made head and eye movements toward the serving table in front of her and Margaret—rather comically indicating the reason for her "rudeness" lay there. An also almost empty bottle of Bailey's B&B. "Smells so nice in here."

She next made a peculiar little body motion, then a barely audible sound Leiv wasn't quite sure what it was. But he questioned himself, *did Adeleine just burp?*

She brought her hand to her mouth and made another face. "Oops. Sorry. I'm not much of a drinker."

Next to her, Margaret Deers smiled broadly, then chuckled a bit herself before reaching over and patting Adeleine's spandex-slacks covered knee. "You've had a long day, dear."

Glover's lucky to have a mother like Margaret, Leiv thought as he watched the two women interact. He could easily imagine why his father took a fancy to her "back in the day" before meeting his mother, Sophie.

"It took me several minutes to actually see them," Adeleine continued, evidently undaunted by her claimed booze-fog. "Even when Hester pointed right at them. Two satellites and a nested kind of apartment in the center. Staircase hidden behind a wall in the carriage house." She finished in a tone of awe, "What an interesting man your grandfather was." Then she smiled rather goofily, and stared at Leiv.

It took Leiv several long minutes to realize Adeleine wasn't talking about locating a box of Moser antique liquor glasses. Rather, she was now talking about his sneakily hidden away satellite disks—TV and Internet—and the small apartment he'd forgot about built into LC's carriage house. He hadn't been in the apartment in ages, but did remember it had a fairly nice second floor view. Nothing like his five-sided copula way up top—but decent enough.

Finally, after catching up, Leiv returned her smile. "We got lucky there with the satellites. 'We' being the installers, and me kibitzing. Had to be pointing south, and at some angle I can't remember. Happened to work out we could squeeze them between those two front turrets on the left when you're looking up."

"Don't see the dishes on top of my office either. That front façade on Main Street hides them," Glover contributed from the rocker squeezed in to Leiv's right. "For all practical purposes, looking at Shiné as a whole, wouldn't think we're 'connected' at all."

"And our transmitters are camouflaged as trees," Leiv added, remembering Pete Lily's aerial video of the Mojave. "I remember him asking about cell phone reception. How he was getting it out here."

Leiv still remembered the spring night in this very withdrawing room. Bittersweet goodbyes—and then the big reveal of David Milhouse and Hester Miller's romantic connection. *One of those great mysteries of love.* Unconsciously, he shook his head slightly—still in wonderment.

The rocker Glover was now sitting in was the only change to LC's withdrawing room since the movie-making crew sendoff.

The armless parlor chair was a last minute accommodation for the number of people that night—and makeshift for sure. A place to fit Glover in the group. Since then, the Chief had taken to the spot next to Leiv, but not taken to the chair.

Consequently, Glover searched the castle—top to bottom including all the bedrooms on both sides of the grand staircase, and eventually came up with a small antique-looking rocker. Leiv initially thought it too small for Glover's substantial frame. And it did turn out to be a snug fit, indeed. But the little-looking rocker seemed to contour perfectly to his brother's body, and consequently since that first Saturday after the movie maker's goodbye party—"the little rocker," as Leiv still thought of it—with its rather faded upholstery, had worked great.

"Want a refill, Lloyd?" Leiv asked.

The pastor shook his head.

"Think I'll empty the bottle then. I'm sure I have more in the kitchen if it's needed."

After draining the last of the Harvey's bottle into his own diminutive antique glass, Leiv sighed—oblivious to who might hear him. Then he looked around. Two years now—*or is it three*—since his return to Shiné—possibly to stay—and he still took pleasure and comfort from LC's withdrawing room. The massive old-world look and feel of the room continued to strike a chord somewhere within.

He was especially fond of LC's grand stone fireplace and hearth, with its perfectly accompanying Anatolia Terrain Hearth-Rug in front. Tonight, Dobie had returned with Hester and David to take her place on that very rug—albeit if only for the night. He still wished the Doberman had chosen him over Hester. *Pettiness on my part.*

Of course there was the added pleasure of knowing one of LC's Mojave stones was hidden in plain sight—right in the center of the broad rock surface above the fireplace. Telling Glover the truth about the stones was still a needed task remaining undone. *His fault for deserting me this morning.* Remembering, he almost humphed aloud. A local fire and a dead body on I-40 definitely shouldn't preempt his Mojave-Stone revelations. *Pettiness again.*

Adeleine was right, Leiv next reflected—it did smell very nice. The aromas of hors d'oeuvres, liqueurs, and wood burning all combining into a uniquely pleasant fragrance. *A very nice ambiance.* Enjoying the moment, Leiv let his thoughts take a further moment to continue looking around. Sitting straight in front, and the farthest away from him to the left of the fireplace were Mary Jones and Doctor Will Walker—comfortable looking he thought, in their replica Spoon-back chairs centered on one small Victorian end table. To the right of the fireplace were identical Spoon-back chairs and end table. Hermit Chan was in one of those chairs, and tonight, the second chair sat empty. *As if waiting for someone,* Leiv thought whimsically.

It was pleasant seeing Mary sitting smiling and talking to Will. From his past Shiné adventures, Leiv considered her a most unusual and rather psychically-inclined woman. Indeed, there was a special place in his psyche and heart for Mary Jones—their local incognito TV soap opera star. He could see they both held half-filled wine goblets, but couldn't hear what they were saying to each other. He wondered. *Romance?*

Leiv did hear Glover say sotto voce to his right, "I need to talk to you before I go. Alone."

Leiv nodded, and thought, *so do I, dear brother.*

Tonight's room seating was oval as usual—a setup Hester had arranged in his early days entertaining in LC's withdrawing room. Well, he thought, at first it was a small "U," when Pastor Lloyd Apply, Doctor Will Walker, and Glover's mother Margaret Deers mutually agreed it would be nice getting together once a week. There was for sure, a bit of rollover from Everett's days at Rhodes Castle, and even earlier in LC's time. Leiv, for his part, just made the arrangement more official with his friends. Every Saturday night. And with increasing numbers like Glover, the "U" evolved to become larger and quite definite—especially when trying to accommodate the movie crew.

Tonight, Adeleine had clandestinely set up the same two-table food arrangement in the center of his oval. He guessed, according to Hester's instructions. He looked to the loveseat to his right and facing the food tables. Hester and David sat toward Leiv's end, close together and holding hands. They were talking—only to each other it seemed, and looking rather goofily happy. *Marriage just a week away.*

Elizabeth May sat to the other end of the same loveseat. It wasn't that tight of a fit for the lovebirds and her—for it was a long loveseat. That particular couch, if he remembered correctly, was an addition to the room from his father Everett. *Big and pricey.*

Earlier today, at her request, Leiv left Adeleine in the kitchen—wanting, she said, to be alone with another cup of one of Hester's awful teas. He had moved on to lock back, front, and garage doors securely, planning to next retreat to his library sanctum.

For, as her unofficial caretaker, he needed to figure out what "to do" about Adeleine. Hester had already shown her the guest room, which was still stocked with towels and necessities. And on leaving her as she started making herself more tea, he did suggest she take a nap. Leiv was sure at the time she wouldn't take his advice. Indeed, as he headed upstairs to his library, Leiv heard continued clinking and clanking noises in the kitchen.

He *now* knew what her plan was. He looked to the tables, then over at her. Once again she was watching him.

"Kudos," he praised her with an accompanying little dip of the head acknowledgement. *And quite a strong woman on another front,* he thought—*holding up quite well, considering a hit man was on her trail.* Indeed, Adeleine had prepared a bunch of sandwich-rectangles and quiche-like finger food things in addition to Hester's usual. And David, he now knew, had picked up the pizza slices from TGS Tavern. Chef Jack was very proud of the brick pizza oven he'd added out back. And though not the best pizzas Leiv had ever tasted, they were getting better every time he tried one.

"He's still alive!" A loud male voice from the withdrawing room hallway entrance announced with excitement, relief, and over-the-top dramatic emphasis. The news bearer was Walker Johns, Shiné ambulance technician, part time deputy, and volunteer firefighter. He stood in the fashion of a town crier with his arms stretched wide.

LC's great room went quiet. Expectant. All their combined attention focused on Walker.

"It was touch and go there for awhile." Walker stepped farther into the room as he continued his announcement, moving around the back of Mary Jones and Will Walker and toward the center of the fireplace. He turned his head from side to side to take in everyone, and made different arm and hand gestures Leiv couldn't quite interpret. He thought they were mainly expressions of jubilant excitement.

Then Walker focused his eyes on Glover and Leiv, his occasional boss and the man whose drawing room he was now standing in. He was clearly still excited, and talking louder than required—even for the large size of the room. "Sorry, your front door was unlocked and I thought you'd want to hear about Lucca. And you weren't answering your phone, Chief."

Leiv stood up. He wanted to go to the excited looking young man.

Walker held up his right hand. "It's okay, Mr. Rhodes." His voice was calmer and lower. "I don't want to bust up your party. I was just so relieved. When that doctor came in and said he was breathing okay. Normal like..." He took a deep breath, clearly trying to calm himself further. "...I really thought he was going to die this morning."

Leiv moved to his left, and almost tripped over Lloyd who was in the middle of also getting up. From behind him to his right, he heard additional movement-like noises—Glover he guessed.

But to his amazement Leiv saw that before any of them could get to Walker—Adeleine had already gotten up and swiftly moved to the young man's side. Once close to him and within seconds, she slid one arm into his and the other touching his back lightly. "Here, Sir, sit down in this chair." She nudged him toward the empty Spoon-back chair next to Hermit Chan—who also seemed to be in the process of getting up to help. *Ironic and right.* Leiv thought. *Help for the volunteer helper extraordinaire.*

Walker sat, smiled, then looked rather sheepish.

Leiv blew out his own deep breath and sat back down himself. Then leaning forward as if it made a difference all the way across the Great-room, said loudly, "What a relief he's alive." Walker's announcement was more of a relief to Leiv than he expected. "He's not alone, right? Jasmine's there with him, right?"

Walker nodded. "And her husband, Timothy."

"Timothy?" In all the time he'd known Lucca and Jasmine, it never crossed his mind she might be married.

"Tim Teague." Lloyd Apply contributed in a tone dripping in self-satisfaction. "I told you tomorrow will be interesting with Tim there."

Projecting across the large room, Walker said, "Maybe you haven't met him. Mr. Teague's father was a big time nudist. Left his franchise to Tim."

But before Leiv could explore further this amazing revelation, Leiv watched Adeleine put a wine glass in Walker's hand and place a small plate of goodies on the table next to him. Then he heard Walker mumble after taking a hefty swallow of wine and nabbing an *hors d' oeuvre*, "Lucca's going to be okay. I just know he will."

Convincing himself, Leiv figured. Sort of a prayer-mantra, and Leiv guessed Walker had been reciting those phrases all day.

What a day this has been. Yet, now, tonight, after another one of those longest of days—we're congenially sitting around drinking. As if nothing horrible happened right across the road. As if Lucca wasn't in the hospital, fighting to hold on to his life. As if a dead body hadn't been found on I-40. As if....

He forced his mind in yet another direction. Toward Adeleine's father. Obviously, something Winston had said or done to the wrong person was the catalyst for him having to bring his daughter across country from Illinois to California for safety reasons. Were any of today's happenings connected to that? He couldn't imagine how they could be.

"Winston," he said aloud before catching himself.

"What did you say?" Pastor Apply asked.

"Nothing, nothing," Leiv answered quickly. "Just mumbling." Leiv had let his mind and emotions indulge themselves in the old-days and old-dislikes.

Everyone else now seemed back into their own conversations, even Glover was now talking past Hester and David to Elizabeth-May on the love seat to his right. Looked like Hermit was engaging Walker in conversation—and rather lively, if hand gestures were taken into account. Adeleine had returned to her seat and was talking with Lloyd and Margaret about some meeting tomorrow morning.

Yes, he figured he could continue his self-indulgent wallow in retrospective meanderings a bit longer. A waste of time when it came to living a happy life, Leiv figured—but sometimes it just felt good to rehash, re-accuse, and even sometimes—regret. Especially when it came to Winston.

Unfortunate and unkind as the truth was, Leiv knew he never really liked Winston Moore—only tolerated him. However, with the passage of time back then, he finally arrived at a point of acceptance—enough at least that he could work with him. Had to actually—Winston had his fingers in so many political pies.

Political pies he had to constantly ignore—or when pressed for results, work his way through.

On the good side—Leiv looked over at Adeleine, and saw she was smiling and still chatting with Margaret and the pastor during what was turning out to be a pleasant enough evening given the day's circumstances. *She's weathering this adventure quite well.* Especially knowing she was a bull's-eye on someone's target.

He eavesdropped enough to hear, "Oh, no," as Adeleine was telling Margaret with emphasis, "Illinois cornfields are nothing like this part of California." Her mannerisms, her phraseology, her looks were very much like her mother's— Penny. Now deceased, but when alive, Leiv remembered being continually amazed at her tolerance for Winston. *Loved him, I think.*

And from what he'd seen so far of Adeleine—standing side by side with her youthful personality was the capacity for introspection. And kindness. He knew it was a lot of assumptions to make in one day—but there it was. *Funny that.* And once again his mind returned to her father Winston. *Unresolved dissatisfactions*, he figured.

"And his eyes," a law clerk had once confided to Leiv, "they only connect in a salesman-type way." Leiv forced himself not to smile now, remembering Winston was the main mover in proposing his own name, then later Leiv's name instead, for the next Illinois Supreme Court vacancy. He knew it was because Winston had been offered something bigger. Governor nomination, maybe?

He sighed audibly, wondering what Winston had gotten himself into this time.

From Leiv's left, Lloyd broke off his talking with the two ladies and intruded himself into his meanderings down memory lane. "Like I've already warned, you. Don't be surprised, Leiv," he was saying in his most superior pastor-like tone, "at what you hear at the community meeting." He paused for a couple seconds. "Or the people you meet. Like Lucca's husband. If you got out more. Especially if you came to church."

"Say no more, Lloyd. I deserve whatever surprises I get." Leiv gestured with open-palmed hands. "I'll be counting on you to be my guide."

"We'll be saying some prayers for Lucca before the 'business' meeting." He said the word *business* with uncensored distaste.

Leiv definitely was not looking forward to the community meeting at Shiné Church's meeting room Sunday. But tonight was too nice to spoil with details about tomorrow.

From his right, Glover said again he wanted some alone time with Leiv before leaving. "Can we talk for a few minutes? I'd like to fill you in on I-forty."

Leiv nodded agreeably, both men stood, and walked to the back corner of the withdrawing room under the pretense of Leiv showing Glover the antique floor lamp standing in the corner. Three aperitifs of Harvey's Bristol Crème had worked their magic and taken the edge off any lingering animosity towards Glover from this morning's desertion at TGS. The sherry had also prepared him, Leiv figured, for whatever shenanigans Shiné's Community Church could come up with tomorrow. *It's a church for goodness' sakes.* What could possible happen at a church meeting?

Of course Leiv knew by morning, there would be nothing left of his "Harvey's glow." If anything, he might have a headache.

Once in the corner, Glover said, leaning in closer to him and lowering his voice, "I think I've got a dead hit man lying on a slab in the Needles morgue."

Could this hit man been coming after Adeleine? Leiv's interest was now definitely piqued as he listened intensely as Glover explained about the morning call from Ben disturbing their breakfast, and his office confab with the two Needles deputies.

Leiv interrupted once to say, "I suggested you get that printer."

When Glover finished, he then sat quietly.

"What a day," Leiv eventually said aloud.

"Yeah," Glover agreed without hesitation.

"And where the heck do you guys come up with these monikers?"

Glover chuckled. "The names come with the bulletins," he said, sidestepping Leiv's question.

"Do you have a name-the-criminal book like they do for baby names?"

Glover's chuckle morphed into a full guffaw. "I think you've overdone it on the Harvey's." He leaned forward a bit and made a head gesture back toward the empty bottle on the table between Leiv and Lloyd's chairs.

"Our pastor can really put it away," Leiv sassed back.

Everyone who was leaving, left.

Rhodes Castle was quiet again.

But the evening was not over for Leiv. After escorting Adeleine to her guest bedroom and still in his withdrawing room attire—with the exception of exchanging his smoking jacket for his special lined hoodie—and like a silent apparition in his movements, Leiv exited through the front door, making sure he locked it soundly behind him. Leiv then slipped around back of the castle, and headed down the path to LC's secret cave.

The moon was bright against a clear and almost black Mojave night-sky. Still, several times at spots he knew could be treacherous, Leiv turned on his flashlight for a few seconds to illuminate the trail ahead.

And once inside, it wasn't long before he was sitting in his *special* chair, *specially* positioned, inside the damp-darkness of LC's hillside cave. His flashlight was off—Leiv didn't need physical illumination to caress the aged diary resting in his lap. The feel of the diary's worn leather cover was a bridge across the years in the quiet chilly darkness.

Leigh-Everett Rhodes said within himself, to himself, and to his grandfather Lee Cooper Rhodes, *as long as I'm able, I will take care to preserve your wishes.* Then he wondered why he'd made such a promise.

Once again, LC's cave took on a surreal, almost mystical nature. What generational wish was he anticipating needed protecting? And from what?

He shivered, and his thoughts prompted him not to stay and commune with LC for long. He wasn't sure what LC was trying to tell him—but his own senses told him not to leave Adeleine alone for long. That was one protecting job he already knew about.

At the same time, for some reason, Leiv also knew he needed to return here soon.

Chapter Four
Too Many Pawns

From LC's journal: Don't know why I write all this stuff down. Guess I'm a hoping someday my scribbling will connect with somebody. Especially a Rhodes, or whatever the name changes to by then.

Sunday Morning:

Okay, there was still dust blowing around a bit—but once again, Ben could not deny it was another outstanding morning sunrise. In a better frame of mind than yesterday, he chalked this morning's particular dichotomy up on his mental blackboard to "everything" has a good side. *Even the Mojave.*

An example for a dog lover like himself was, that heinous criminals sometimes, even the worst of scumbags—quite often loved and spoiled their dogs. Which brought on a smile, thinking about Prince, his own beloved Dalmatian, enjoying the doggie-good-life with his well-paid babysitter. Probably running around Mrs. Quinels's backyard with her other charges this very moment. And boy, did that dog love to ride in his truck, strapped into the seat next to him—as if he was a person.

CHP Officer Ben Bellaeu had always liked driving—all the way back to his teenage years. Indeed, he still remembered with the romantic nostalgia only time provides—his dad patiently driving around with him after receiving his learner's permit. With their dog at the time, Champ, in the backseat.

Liking driving was in fact one of the reasons Ben elected to try for the highway patrol versus any of the various city police units, or the county sheriff's department. *And the TV shows*—such exciting chases. He knew they were stunts, but still. He sighed into the quiet of his cruiser.

Nowadays, the childlike notion of cruising California's extensive interstate and intra state roadways enjoying the scenery and prestige seemed quite silly. But the notions of helping motorists in distress and spotting criminals listed on "Be On the Lookout" bulletins, remained psychological driving forces for him. Even dealing with the horrendous mess in Cajon Pass yesterday—in honest retrospect, the experience gave him a feeling of fulfillment as a CHP officer.

There was also the responsibility to give tickets for driving or vehicle infractions, which was his least favorite part of the job. That reality check brought another sigh, and a shifting of his position in his seat.

Sadly, this morning he was reduced to sitting in one of his favored "ticket giving" spots—in back of a concrete overpass pillar. This particular hideaway, combined with its easy access from the median to head out into southwest or northeast lanes, was perfect. He would rather be doing something else, but no callouts, no BOLOS, no Caltrans construction work this Sunday—nothing he could even tenuously volunteer for.

Even though Ben could see minor dust-devils dancing down the median strip, he lowered his window half an inch or so. With his window closed, he had enjoyed quiet, dust free air. Calmness. A cocoon. But there was something about this morning's air he also found compelling. A unique freshness only available in early in the day hours that he usually didn't take time to appreciate. Once his passenger side window was open a smidgeon, the hum of steadily moving traffic also wafted in with his sought after morning air.

Nice. Ben smiled again. Even though he didn't expect to issue many citations—he knew from the brake lights he saw come on as vehicles passed and saw him for the first time—just his presence was slowing traffic down to near the speed limit.

He also liked this morning's particular spot, because if you *had* to be out in the hither regions of San Bernardino County on I-15 duty, one of his favorite breakfast haunts was nearby. Usually, some Sheriff's Deputies he knew would be hanging out at the back table, and this morning especially, he hoped to maybe pick up something useful. In chorus with his latest thoughts, Ben's stomach growled, and he fondly figured his dog Prince was having his breakfast about now. *Time for me to eat too.*

For some reason, Mugs Nightshade liked Barstow. *Sort of.* In truth, he had only been there two times—both both times staying at Route 66 signed hotels that were nicely priced, clean, and convenient to what he called quick getaway highways. I-40 and I-15. And there was some history to the place, he'd even walked through a Route 66 Museum and a Train Museum in something called a Harvey House.

Even last night before falling off, he thought about how this Barstow place connected to Chicago. Prompting him to spend some more time thinking about his grandmother on Paulina Street, and Uncle Henry on Hoyne Avenue—wondering why they stayed in the city; while others in their generation headed out. *Westward bound.* California even. He knew why he stayed. He loved Chicago. Its history, its feel, its rhythm of changing neighborhoods. He would never forget going shopping on Milwaukee Avenue with Uncle Henry.

Now this Sunday morning, years later and actually on the West Coast, Mugs sat on the edge of his motel room bed, the blinds shut tight trying to fend off that awful rising desert sun blaring in his window, *and* trying to decide how to handle this

Moore person. Mugs had taken to using "person" versus "woman." He sighed, which surprised him.

Then his stomach growled. Not a surprise.

Then, out of the blue it felt like, Mugs remembered a little restaurant he ate at while making his desert-exit-plan last time.

"Just last spring." He shook his head at his continuing desert regret. "And here I am, back in this damn desert again."

The place he recalled was small, right off of I-15 near a hotel, on the side of the highway heading to Vegas. The way he needed to head—though it was too early to head out yet.

"Penny's." *Funny I remember the name.* Actually, he did know why the name stayed tucked away in his memory. Mugs had a girlfriend named Penny—*way back when*. Still in high school he was then—him at St. Ignatius, and her at Providence.

Not that it was easy having girlfriends with them Jesuits and my buttinsky relatives watching my every move.

While falling asleep Saturday night, Leiv thought about spending his Sunday morning early hours in LC's copula. Even after last night's "too long" of a Saturday night get-together, and his short visit to LC's cave, he still planned on rising early to do what he needed to do.

For sure, his cave-visit last night had been unsettling. He'd needed—felt compelled actually—to come back this morning. Predawn. Before Adeleine got up. Rhodes Castle was again locked up well. He'd made sure of that. And Adeleine was still asleep—he'd also checked on that.

Now, Sunday morning and he was back sitting in LC's cave-chair. Fully awake, though cold and anxious. *Waiting for something? Waiting for answers to questions he had yet to pose.*

Leiv did know he wanted the cave to remain in darkness. A blackness through which he could communicate with his grandfather.

But his eyes caught a flicker? *A flash of something.*

It was too dark in the cave for a reflection, and he hadn't lit any of three antique oil lamps strategically placed in the small area. Yet something on the wall directly in front of LC's cave chair had caught Leiv's eye with light of some kind.

No, he negated the existence of whatever he thought he might have seen, and stretched his body out farther, letting himself metaphorically melt into his grandfather's Eames chair. *Forget the flash.* Leiv forced his eyes closed. *I won't be able to fantasize flickers on cave walls with my eyes shut.*

He let his mind ramble at will.

Most mornings these days, and especially on Sundays, watching Shiné sunrises develop usually called him. No matter how tired he might be from the night before. *Yes,* LC's especially designed five-sided cupola with its generous windows and window seats at the very top of Rhodes Castle often beckoned him first. Yet here he was this morning—after very few hours of sleep, trying to communicate with his ancestor during his special predawn copula time. *In the dark.*

Next in Leiv's usual morning ritual would be time spent in LC and Everett's library—*now mine.* Though he still remained reticent to claim the room as his. From the Castle's library he would yet again enjoy the later developing full colors of most Shiné sunrises. Before Hester's departure, he would then head to the kitchen—usually only her domain except for Sunday mornings—where Leiv would fix himself pancakes or French toast. Sometimes he'd head off to TGS for Chef Jack's French toast, but not often.

I planned yesterday's breakfast with Glover well in advance. He sighed.

Even now, here in his grandfather's cave, the library ambiance washed over him for a moment, with its old-world-comfortableness and rich adornments. At this point in his Shiné sojourn, the copula and library were combining into one in Leiv's mind—and were the heart of LC's monument. In both places, Leiv felt like he could reach out to him across the years.

Though here in the cave lay his strongest connection to his grandfather.

With his eyes still closed, Leiv fancied he heard LC say, *"Get my gun."* His eyes shot open and he shook his head hard. Leiv quickly rationalized the voice by telling himself he'd fallen into a semi-dream state for a second.

Yet even with his eyes now wide-open, Leiv heard more, *"Keep it with you. Danger."*

Leiv looked to his lap, LC's "real" diary, *not the one Hester thought she'd stolen,* was there—his right hand pressing against its cool and damp-feeling leather. He grasped the diary tightly, then placed it on the makeshift crate-table to his right.

Figuring he needed to pull himself back into the real world fast, Leiv said in a much louder than his normal tone, as if he was actually talking to whomever or whatever was spooking him, "I need to make breakfast for Adeleine," *I have a houseguest.* "And HM is not here to cook for her," he added in a more somber and softer tone. Physically marking what he knew to be his present physical reality.

What the hell am I doing? Actually talking to ghosts? He was not an "other realities" man. Connecting to LC over the generations was one thing, but hearing a voice was a little much. Hoping to clear his mind, Leiv forced his thoughts elsewhere— landing back on his latest spoken words—Hester Miller.

To be truthful, despite her cantankerous nature, Gypsy heritage-script, and general "steal the Mojave-stone" skullduggery—he missed her.

These days, when HM, David, and Dobie weren't camping on their land south of the castle—which Leiv was planning on giving them as a wedding present—Hester and Dobie often went along to wherever David Milhouse's current production site was. Eating catered breakfasts, Leiv visualized. With plenty of treats for Dobie he also figured. Leiv smiled at that imagery and wondered if HM enjoyed being waited on. *Probably not.* Nonetheless, *he* was glad HM was being waited on for once—and simultaneously missed her even more.

"*Get the gun,*" he thought he heard the voice call out again from the blackness of the cave.

"Grandfather?" he barely whispered—then immediately felt like a fool. *I'm a retired Judge, for goodness sake.*

"*Get the gun.*"

Then the flicker on the wall straight ahead flashed again.

Leiv pushed himself up from LC's Eames Chair, and stumbled forward in pitch blackness to where he thought he'd seen the flicker of light.

His hand felt cave wall. Cold, but not wet. Then metal. *A handle?* Even colder.

He pulled, and a tiny strong box easily responded to his tug—as it had been waiting for him. *Maybe forty-some years?*

Leiv searched in his jean's pocket for his LED penlight, turned it on, and placed the light between his teeth pointing at the box. With both hands now free, Leiv opened the lid without effort. *No rust?*

Inside, looking almost like it had been freshly cleaned and oiled was a gun—wrapped in an aged red paisley bandana. A Colt .45.

He thought he recognized the gun. A gun his father Everett had shown him when he was just a child. *How can I remember this gun?* Leiv wasn't sure how old he actually was at the time, but it was before they headed to Chicago. *But remember I do.* Down to the detail of his father explaining it was a M1911 without a safety.

Adeleine didn't know what to think about her current circumstances, and barely knew how she felt. In fact, she was experiencing an odd duality—of feeling like a child once again, while simultaneously knowing she was more in control of her own life than ever before.

Still predawn, but she was wide awake and wiggled around comfortably in her gigantic bed. Then she fluffed one of the multitudinous pillows across the head of the bed and exchanged the one directly behind her head with a new fluffier one. The pillows felt "modern" and to her taste—filled with some special polyester foam filling, she guessed. Not the down-feather ones she'd expected—and was glad they weren't. She rolled her head back and forth in her newly chosen pillow's fluffiness—while contrarily musing that down-pillows were probably more appropriate to the room's ambiance.

Yes, part of her confusion she supposed, was her new surroundings—and the atmosphere exuding from this unique Shiné world she found herself in. From the castle turrets and top to bottom stained glass entryway, to this—the guest bedroom. Now *her* bedroom—*but for how long?*

Leiv and Hester had explained the monstrous four-poster bed she was sleeping in was his grandfather, LC's. And the room's last occupants were his cousins, a Sydney and Nadya Collins. Last winter, she thought she remembered him saying. The Judge also hinted there was an interesting story involved with their visit back then, and he would fill her in sometime.

Wonder what story will be told about my visit down the road? A sad or a happy tale? She'd wondered the same thing last night before finally drifting off to sleep. Evidently, still of interest to her emotions this morning.

Leiv did take the time to also say Sydney fell in love with Rhodes Castle. From the British royalty-evoking high ceilings, all the meticulously created stained glass windows, the extravagant amount of square footage, the excellently chosen antiques— Sydney claimed he felt at home the moment he stepped through the massive front entry doors. Nadya, Leiv added, "Not so much," then left it at that. Adeleine was sure there was more left to be told about their visit.

She also liked the huge four-poster herself, and particularly the chest bed-seat spanning the bed's foot. There were also several massive armoires, two armchairs, and thick rugs. And an *en suite* bathroom even. From the style and look of the place, she had expected a water-closet down the hall.

Further luxuriating under her layers of quilt, and with follow-on consideration, Adeleine concluded she very much liked this room. But could she stay here in this dust-bowl very long?

No, she really couldn't imagine a life here.

Though the reddish-orange mix of colors she saw trying to peek above her windowsill, were quite unique. Enticing even. But not enticing enough for her to get up and go investigate. Besides, she guessed it was probably rather cold outside her quilt cocoon. The fireplace wasn't lit. Was there central heating? *Oh my.* But there was electricity, she probably just needed to find and drag a heater into the room. She was sure Judge Rhodes would not go without the comfort of heat in the winter.

"Sure hope they find that damn hit man soon," she told the room she was becoming rather fond of.

Another part of her confusion, Adeleine knew, was her father. Sure, she led a semi-independent life back in Illinois, her own apartment, career, men friends—and handled all the circumstances her "independent" situation entailed. But father was never more than a two-hour drive away—usually less. And though they often butted heads, he was there for her. *Backup for her.*

But now, he'd screwed up royally someway, somehow— and was now trying to get her out of harm's way. In a nutshell, he loved her—and also remained her life's backup. They would be almost two-thousand miles away from each other. She needed to *really* grow up. And fast.

Funny, Adeleine thought she should have been excited and eager—as was her usual inclination toward life. Instead, she felt—well, Adeleine wasn't quite sure what she felt. *Trepidation? Fear?*

Yes, she settled on her answer. *I'm scared.*

It was still early when Leiv rang Adeleine's bedroom on the house phone. Something HM liked doing instead of walking upstairs. Adeleine picked up immediately and sounded delighted at his offer of special Sunday morning breakfast. There was plenty of time, he figured, for them to eat before heading off to Lloyd's church service at Shiné Community Church proper, and then the follow-on community meeting in the connected assembly room annex.

Leiv was also still unnerved by his predawn cave experience, and intuitively thought having breakfast with Adeleine would tell him if he'd gone cuckoo or not. Not necessarily unhinged because he'd somehow spied a gun hidden in the cave's wall—for he *did* have a real physical gun in his possession—but that a voice from the past had told him where to look for said gun. *Definitely cuckoo.*

Now, very few slices of French toast remained on the platter sitting in the center of the kitchen table. The serving dish was his mother Sophie's Spode Blue Italian oval platter he had lugged along with his law books back to Rhodes Castle from Chicago. It was now empty enough of toast to reveal what Leiv thought its "pretty nice" pattern—to use HM's words. For him, its value was sentimental. *A piece of my mother through a possession she loved.*

Savoring his last mouthfuls of French toast, Leiv knew that if he were alone, he would be sighing with satiated pleasure. Maybe even patting his stomach. Something he'd done more than once in the past. Usually at TGS when hidden away in the back booth, but occasionally also after his own cooking if he were alone. Now, having a house guest, "things" were different.

He asked Adeleine abruptly, "Are you scared of guns?"

"Of course not," she answered in a tone indicating it was a silly question, especially coming from him.

On second thought, he realized her tone of voice was quite appropriate—it was a silly question. He knew Adeleine was born and raised in Illinois farmland, where the standard child raising practice included teaching your children how to handle a rifle and a shotgun—even a pistol. *At least it used to be in my day.* He wondered if farm-culture was still the same? A question Leiv couldn't remember ever before considering. "Are farm ways still the same?"

Adeleine was mid-chew, savoring *her* last bites it looked like, and consequently took her time answering. Finally, "Pretty much. And this is a great breakfast, by the way. Not only was the French toast great, but my eggs were cooked just the way I like them." She made eye and head movements toward his mother's serving dish. "And that platter is gorgeous."

Leiv felt his face warm.

She gave him a teasing look. "Who taught you—" Then quickly catching herself, her expression immediately turned somber. Then Adeleine brought a hand to her mouth for a few seconds in embarrassment. "I'm so sorry, Judge. I forgot you'd lost your wife." She took a heavy breath. "In a horrible traffic accident in Chicago? Right?" She didn't wait for him to respond. "I even remember her name. Melissa Mays." She waited a few seconds—then looking a bit more composed, asked in a soft tone, "Melissa taught you how to cook. Right?"

Leiv smiled—hoping to banish her embarrassment—then nodded. Why not let Adeleine give Melissa credit for any perceived cooking skills she thought he had? Truth was, his mother and grandmother taught him the few things he knew about kitchens and culinary doings.

During his grieving later days as a bachelor again, cooking didn't exist—*me alone still in Chicago.* Eating times were populated with Vienna Dogs from the corner stand, Italian Beef sandwiches only a mile away, Cantonese restaurants in every city neighborhood he lived in. *The pizza boxes would probably stack up to even the castle's high ceilings —*

"What are you thinking about?" Adeleine broke into his reverie. "You looked like you were miles away."

"I was. Sucked up into years gone by."

She smiled. "You sound like you're old as Methuselah, and fallen into spouting off old-geezer wisdom."

Leiv laughed. Couldn't not. Then after a moment, he cleared his throat, straightened himself in his hard-backed spindle chair and leaned in a little across the kitchen table. "I have a gun in the house. I'll be keeping it close until all this blows over."

"Good," she said without pause or need for consideration. "What father finally let on near the end before dumping me..." She held up her hand, "No protestation needed, I know he was thinking about protecting me. Ah...back to what I was starting to say, what I took from some of his parting comments was this guy was dangerous. 'Nasty piece of work' to use one of Father's favorite phrases."

She looked so young to his "Methuselah-eyes," yet there she was, quite maturely taking in the world as it was in a surprisingly wise manner.

"Do you still have time for coffee before you leave?" she asked.

"Yes." He made a move to get up.

She beat him to it. "I'll do it. I like my coffee strong." She turned back toward him for a second before getting up, "Or would you prefer a cup of tea. I found another can on the shelf that said 'Tea,' and smelled quite interesting. Spicy."

"Sounds good," he absently agreed to the tea instead of coffee. His attention had jumped elsewhere—for out of nowhere, LC's otherworldly cave voice caught Leiv by surprise again. *Danger,* loud and clear. But in his ears only, he was sure. Then the word shouted in his head for a second time. *Danger.* And he didn't think it had anything to do with the tea.

He was certain—the red-flag voice was waving for danger coming Adeleine's way.

Quickly, Leiv forced his attention back to his houseguest. "I think you should go with me to the church. Is that okay?" He hoped his tone was light. Nonchalant.

"Yep, I'd love to see what desert folks are like." She was now at the kitchen sink behind him.

Leiv continued to sit, waiting for his tea, and taking the time to assess this morning all over again. Particularly, how he felt about possible risks now intruding into his world.

In particular, he wondered why Winston thought he was the right person to protect his daughter. *I certainly wouldn't have driven across the country to drop my daughter off—if I had one—with someone I hadn't seen in several years.* Just because Winston thought he was a good Illinois Supreme Court nominee, didn't automatically make him a good guardian. A caretaker of your daughter's life? Well, he would definitely keep an eye on her— and he was sure Glover would help if he asked. But what did Winston see in him he didn't know about? Maybe it was as simple as the remoteness of Shiné?

Glover had seemed quite interested last night in the why and wherefore of Adeleine's appearance on his doorstep. *Maybe he knew something?* More face to face time with his half-brother was definitely needed. For now, he wanted to head to Shiné Community Church soon. Lloyd would never forgive him if on one of the few times he attended service, he arrived late.

But before leaving, he would drink the cup of tea Adeleine was setting in front of him. It had a very rich-looking dark tan color, and the aroma was quite nice. But it tasted terrible. Still, he smiled and gulped it down.

Chapter Five
Board in Disarray

From LC's journal: Some people just can't never agree. Found that out a coming out here. Just thinking about themselves I believe. Land squabbles in particular it seems. Fussing, fighting, even a shoot out I heard. Well, not here in my Shiné. Ain't gonna let none of that happen here. That fancy lawyer got the plotting papers all setup just right. Ain't nothing gonna happen without a Rhodes signing too. Course there were all the good things, all the people who helped build this town. Can't name em all here.

Still Sunday morning:

Pastor Lloyd Apply gave a low-key sermon on "acts of kindness," which Leiv thought was quite well thought out and presented excellently—combining Christian directives and current real world dilemmas and situations. He was proud of his friend's special gift, and for not the first time, thought Lloyd was one of the lucky individuals where "gift" and "calling" fit together quite nicely.

Wished I liked coming to church more often. Unfortunately, Leiv knew he didn't feel comfortable in "congregation" environments. Never had, even as a child. And even though he wished differently—in his heart-of-hearts he knew he would continue spending most Sunday mornings communing with Shiné sunrises and LC for as long as he remained in Shiné.

Also, and not for the first time when he ventured out into the Pastor's domain, Leiv was surprised anew by the number of people who called Shiné Community Church "their church." This time, though, there was the added surprise of the number of people who cared about the community—indeed, felt they had a stake in Shiné happenings and its future.

Who are all these people, Leiv asked himself?

Of course he knew how many deeds he'd signed off, thanks to LC's codicil on all the land deeds he had initially claimed in the 1930s. His father Everett, of course, had signed off many before Leiv's arrival at Rhodes Castle. Nonetheless, it hadn't registered in Leiv's psyche how many people called Shiné home.

He sent praise to his grandfather across the ages. *You've done good, LC.*

Now the actual church service part was over, and all these folks—he roughly guessed thirty or so in number—seemed to know what was next on the agenda, and where to go. The church annex it looked like, and he and Adeleine moved with the crowd heading that way.

Once over the doorway threshold between church and community center, Adeleine stopped to talk to a man just inside the meeting room door, while Leiv moved on to find a perfect "take it all in" spot away from the meeting tables. His thought was to watch, not participate. *Why?* He wasn't yet sure why he felt the need to hide out. *And what was he watching out for? A threat to Adeleine?* Highly unlikely, he scolded his emotions. *We're in Shiné Community Church for goodness sakes.*

Before getting far toward what looked like a perfect little nook he spotted near the door to the kitchen, Leiv heard Adeleine lie to the man she was talking to. "I'm a visiting relative. Wanted to see how cousin Leigh-Everett was faring."

"Today's a big deal, you know." The man's voice was one he didn't recognize.

"Why? What's happening?" Hearing her from a little distance, and from his rear, Adeleine sounded to Leiv like she was actually interested. He turned around to see what her face was saying, and *yes*, Adeleine looked as curious as her voice implied.

As Leiv headed toward the perfect hideout spot he just spied, the man's face unexpectedly took him back to an Illinois courtroom scenario he would always carry with him. Indeed, there were several similarly imprinted remembrances and images Leiv's mind wouldn't let go of—despite the growing passage of time.

But his "Josh" memory was one of the more vivid ones. Still, knowing all this, Leiv unconsciously shook his head in wonderment that "Josh" was still with him—especially this morning in his developing Shiné life. *His face. His words. His aspect.* Way back then, when he had his own courtroom. *Well, a shared courtroom,* but his own chambers.

During that indelibly remembered trial, "competency" was the legal question with a substantial hunk of agricultural farmland at stake. And during the proceedings, quite unexpectedly in the middle of an opposing family member's statement—Josh, the supposed incompetent heir—though remaining seated at the defense table, had yelled out in a surprisingly loud and commanding voice, "Joy." After a few more seconds and before Leiv fully comprehended what was going on, Josh next yelled, "George." Then raising his arms up high, "Elsa."

Taking it all in back then, Leiv had thought it useless, even a bit inappropriate to gavel the young man's outcries down. And in a short time, courtroom chatter did die down on its own. Though Leiv could also still see the many surprised and bemused faces in the courtroom in front of him.

And Josh had not finished. "Virginia," was his next yell-out.

Even now, Leiv couldn't help smiling, re-watching in his mind's eye Josh then standing up, flinging his arms wide, and starting to sing in an even louder voice, "Born free. Free as the wind blows."

That morning, Leiv's judicial-mind had immediately gone to—*how to shut all this down?* He remembered looking to the guards at the courtroom's three different doors—but before he or they could do anything, *all* the courtroom spectators were on their feet also singing, loudly and in unison with Josh, the lyrics of Born Free. And for many, with their arms held high.

"Mind if I hide out here with you for just a moment?" asked a male voice in the present that he did recognize, and from behind Leiv's right shoulder. "Here, I brought you a cup of the best hot chocolate you'll ever taste."

He knew it was Pastor Lloyd Apply—nonetheless, Leiv was startled—but not enough to spill the offered cup of hot chocolate, which he eagerly turned to receive. Quickly bringing himself back to his present, Leiv said, "I like that you use real ceramic café mugs. Not that Styrofoam stuff." He took a sip, then smiled. Warm, chocolaty-rich, and the perfect temperature. *Much better than that tea this morning.*

Leiv was now standing comfortably ensconced in the corner he found while musing about Josh. A spot where he could still keep an eye on Adeleine as she chatted-on at the entry door with another man he didn't know. *Perfect, actually.* His spot was next to the kitchen's swinging door, and felt just right for a nice little hidey-hole. Nonetheless, despite his clever spot-scoping, Lloyd had succeeded in finding him out. Of course, it *was* Lloyd's church and meeting room. *Probably knows all the nooks and crannies.*

"What were you smiling about?" Lloyd took a couple steps closer into whispering distance of Leiv. He held his mug up to inspection height. "And me too, on the cups that is. These mugs are courtesy of the Route 66 museum at Barstow Harvey House. Fortunately for me, Margaret and Elizabeth-May load them in our kitchen dishwasher after meetings. Not much of big deal for me to unload and stack on the counter for next time." Then after a few seconds' pause as if to make sure Leiv was looking at him and mentally connecting, Lloyd added with a head gesture, "In the kitchen behind us."

Leiv smiled. "I have been here before. You do know that?" He appreciated the circumspectness of Lloyd's various hints over time regarding his lack of church or local function attendance.

"You're right. But I don't remember you being in the hall here since Mayor Oakes's last meeting."

"Has it been that long?"

Lloyd nodded. "Glad you brought Adeleine along too. Nice young woman. Enjoyed the little conversation I had with her last night in LC's withdrawing room. Seems like she's enjoying talking to Tim."

For several long moments, a comfortable silence fell between the two men and as they savored hot chocolate and watched attendees settle in around the two long meeting room tables obviously set up for the occasion.

"A lot has happened since you moved to Shiné," Lloyd finally said. "And keeps on happening." Then he smiled, too. "And you still haven't said what you were laughing about by the way."

"Memories," Leiv said thoughtfully. "You don't really want to hear about 'them olden days.'"

"But I do."

Leiv looked questioningly into Lloyd's eyes for a few seconds and saw genuine curiosity. Consequently, he told the pastor about Josh and that day in court.

"Interesting," Lloyd said when Leiv finished. "Then what happened?"

"We all proceeded to my chambers—"

97

"You had your own chambers? Like on TV?"

Leiv chuckled slightly, and nodded. "Not spacious, or paneled in rich wood like TV and movies tend to make them. But, yes, I had permanent chambers." From the look on Lloyd's face, Leiv thought if it had been part of his friend's character, the pastor would have whistled.

But no, the wise and worldly, but imminently gentle and old fashioned Shiné pastor, just nodded sagely and murmured, "Hmm." But to Leiv, his expression betrayed true amazement. "And what happened in chambers?" Lloyd's tone intimated, "*Do I have to pull every tiny detail out of you?*"

"Actually, I witnessed one of the fastest reversals in my career. The claimants against Josh had a savvy lawyer who knew it would be hard to prove incompetence when an entire courtroom joins you in song. The lawyer told the family and Josh's lawyer in my chambers to drop the whole matter. They did."

"Do you think Josh had mental challenges?"

"Probably." Leiv tilted his head sideways a bit. "But I'm not a shrink. We never got as far as hearing her testimony in court. But personally?" Leiv looked directly into his friend's kind eyes. "Not impaired enough by any means to strip his legal inheritance from him."

"Why did Tim over there make you think of Josh? I saw you were staring at him and Adeleine when I came up."

"Same facial characteristics. Same something...I don't know...turn of the head. Something."

While trying not to look like they were watching them, he and Lloyd both—under cover of sipping hot chocolate—stared for at least a couple more moments at Tim.

After a bit, Lloyd asked *sotto voce*, his lips still hidden by his coffee cup rim, "You know who he is, right?"

Leiv shook his head.

"Jasmine's husband, Timothy Teague. Walker mentioned him last night. Surprised he's come, given the fire and his father-in-law being in the hospital. From what I've heard, Tim's a very smart and canny businessman, so this meeting must be pretty important to him. Margaret, a woman who knows a lot about what goes on around here, told me that at one of your Saturday nights." He humphed slightly. "Though he doesn't really look like the high-flyer businessman type to me."

Leiv smiled, and turned his head a bit so Lloyd wouldn't see his face. *How can Margaret know such a thing?* He liked Glover's mother a lot, *but sometimes*. Though he did think she was rather canny.

Pastor Apply dropped his voice even lower. "As they say, 'books and their covers,' huh? Just like with Josh maybe?"

Leiv thought his friend was being a little judgmental about Tim's casual attire. And contrary to Lloyd, Leiv had also kept the convoluted notion over the years—that just maybe Josh had outsmarted them all.

"Tim's also a nudist. Like his father."

But before Leiv could digest this added little *bon mot*, the pastor shifted gears. "Look," he said in an excited and pleased voice. "It's Walker at the door, maybe with some news about Lucca?"

Leiv's attention was immediately drawn to Walker Johns, and then to Jasmine who within seconds of Walker's entrance, appeared from behind the volunteer firefighter to stand at his side. Leiv also saw Tim then quickly leave Adeleine and head to his wife, Jasmine. Leiv had to push back a glancing thought of what the man might look like without his clothes. Quite surprised; *what the heck's wrong with me?*

Several attendees already gathered in the room also rushed over to Jasmine and Tim as Walker deftly stepped to the side and scanned the room. *Looking for me maybe?* Leiv thought.

Indeed, after a moment or so, Walker caught his eye and headed toward Leiv's hidey-hole.

Lloyd whispered "I'm also off to console Jasmine."

Leiv noticed Adeleine was following right after Walker—also heading toward Leiv. He sighed and said to himself, "So much for being inconspicuous," just as Walker and the quick-walking Adeleine came up to him.

"Was that Pastor Apply I saw rushing through the kitchen?" Walker asked in a questioning voice.

Leiv nodded. "He's off to talk to Jasmine." He swallowed hard thinking about Lucca, then asked Walker the dreaded question, "And how is Lucca doing?"

Walker's tone was somber, "No change." His voice caught, but he immediately recovered. "Still alive, has spoken a couple words a couple of times. But then...but then he relapses. I was so hopeful last night."

Adeleine and Walker had scooted in close to him—and befitting their hideout circumstances, she next added in almost a whisper, "*And*, why are you hiding back here in the corner anyway?"

Leiv tskd—*sounding too much like Glover*. He was feeling a bit boxed in and shifted his weight slightly, trying to accommodate their presence. He'd wanted to take a couple more minutes of quiet time. *Time* to take in the room, so to speak. *No such luck.*

An activity he was good at back in his courtroom days. Unfortunately, near the end of his time on the bench, it was standard procedure to scan for "disruptors"—as one of his politically-sensitive clerks diplomatically liked calling the people Leiv was on alert for. Looking for vengeance seekers, would be terrorists, gang members, and others.

By the time Leiv left Illinois, scanning machines and visual profiling guards were standard fare. Still, several times, not in his courtroom, *thank goodness*, weapons had gotten in and unfortunate incidents almost occurred—except for the quick action of alert guards. Leiv felt himself shaking his head—then realizing he was and quickly looking to his right, he saw Adeleine staring back at him. He smiled.

"Thinking about something in the past?" she intuitively asked.

"Back in the day…"

"It's my father's influence, you know."

"You're right," Leiv agreed. "Winston has brought back memories."

Evidently, also in a world in his own mind, Walker whistled softly—barely audible. "Look at all the people here."

"This isn't usual?" Adeleine asked.

"No way," Walker, a regular church-goer informed her. "Two things going on this morning. Wanting to know about Lucca, and stating their cases for the new county development plan. Shiné gets to input to the plan this go around."

Leiv didn't have a clue what "plan" Walker was talking about. Shiné was LC's town, he was LC's direct heir, a required signee on all Shiné land deals—and was evidently asleep-at-the-switch, as the cliché went. Most land still belonged to LC, *well me now,* and was leased. There had been a few sales, but mostly… Again, he unconsciously shook his head. He remembered a land case maybe five years back—

"Are you doing it again?" Adeleine whispered.

"Indeed I was about to." Leiv took a deep breath, straightened his shoulders, and tried to relax and affix himself in the present. *Darn Winston.* "I think I better pay attention to what's going on here this morning."

Regardless of his resolve, Leiv once again made a quick excursion into his past life. This time re-envisioning Curtis—he couldn't remember his last name—the courtroom artist always sitting up front and drawing participants when newspapers were still an information source, and when Leiv had prohibited camera coverage. Leiv once asked the artist how he captured his subjects the way he did, for he thought Curtis's particular talent was to exaggerate features to a cartoon status, while simultaneously capturing the subject's actual "essence."

"First," Curtis had quite generously explained to him, "I pick the two most prominent features, exaggerate them, but make the others as close as I can to what they really look like. Then I watch for their mannerisms. You know, just like an actor would do if they wanted to define a character. Then I draw my subject in motion, displaying one or more of their typical mannerisms."

Before bringing himself firmly back into his present life — Leiv wondered for the first time during these intervening years — *how would Curtis have drawn me?*

Penny's parking lot was small, easy for CHP Officer Ben Bellaeu to check out who was inside eating. This morning, at the far end of the parking strip right in front of the Airstream-styled restaurant, he saw another CHP black-and-white, a Barstow black-and-white, and two County whites. Ben considered the cruisers a sign his timing was good for obtaining locker room gossip, and hoped these were cops he knew — or at least met already.

Once inside, greetings exchanged — and after he ordered a three egg breakfast platter with orange juice and a small carafe of coffee — Ben was content to listen and learn as his colleagues talked among themselves. He had met them all before, so talk was fairly open, and moved along easily.

"You've heard about the big confab about this new hit man supposedly coming out here?"

"Why is he coming out here to California?"

"Beats me. Haven't heard anything definite on reasons."

"When's the meeting you're going to? And where?"

"Today, in Needles. Brass is guessing he's flying into Vegas then coming across on I-Forty by way of Needles."

"On a Sunday?"

"Yep."

"So, we don't know *why* he's heading to our fair state, but we're speculating on *how*?"

"I know, I know. All I can tell you is that's what I heard this morning at briefing. Which you weren't at." This comment was offered by Ben's fellow CHP officer and specifically to him. "Guessing you were at that accident?"

Ben nodded.

"And helping out in Shiné right?"

Ben nodded again.

"You know all this coffee is going to hit you around Jeremy's on I-15 where there ain't nothing around," the same officer added.

All nodded their heads in wise agreement.

"I know, I know. But the coffee here is damn good. And strong."

When the topic changed from coffee, to movies, then to TV shows that drove them crazy getting cop-stuff wrong—Ben only half listened and finished his breakfast thinking about his own next moves. First off, he wanted to do some computer research on his laptop in his cruiser. Then head out to Shiné.

When he eventually left, his mind racing with to-dos, and under guise of putting on his shades, Ben nonetheless took a good long look at the guy sitting alone at a small booth up front and looking out the window. His instinct told him this guy was purposely trying to make sure Ben didn't notice him.

I've seen that face before. A bulletin maybe? Then he almost laughed out loud at his speculating. *Could have seen him in cousin Celia's wedding album for all I know.* Still, where was the guy's car? Over at the hotel? Was he a guest there? If not, why park where his car wouldn't be noticed?

Then he remembered Cajon Pass. *Same guy? Coincidence?* He needed to check if a rental car was in the lot.

* * * * *

Mugs was so glad he parked his car across the road at the Jack in the Box, in a space half-hidden behind a semi—then he'd walked across Yermo road to the restaurant. Not much "walking around" in the area, but the corner did have a stoplight due to heavy Marine Corp Logistics Base and freeway off-ramp traffic. *Yep,* Mugs considered knowing the lay-of-the-land a key element in being the best hit man around.

Still, all those cops arriving while he was having a second cup of some darned good coffee surprised him—even with his sharp eye for his environment. But Mugs didn't think it a smart move to just get up and leave right after they arrived. *No,* that would have been a dead giveaway. He also prided himself on being smart like that, too. *Won't catch me out that easy*—admittedly though, their popping up during his breakfast in his especially chosen out-of-the-way hideaway had "caught him out." *Later,* he decided, *I'll have to think about what I missed considering.*

And that cop who just left—there was *something* there, though he wasn't sure what that *something* was. He would figure it out. *Have to,* for Mugs didn't like the feeling running down his spine. Based on experience, he trusted his spine to sometimes know stuff before his brain.

Mugs's spine nudged him again. This time transmitting to his brain quite directly—*is this CHP cop going to throw a spanner in the works?*

He wondered. And for the first time since doing-what-he-did, Mugs Nightshade was washed over by a wave of weariness.

Keeping Curtis's remembered drawing techniques in mind, Leiv also added the imagery he was a character in some old-timey golden-age mystery book, looking around the Community Center table and taking in this morning's mostly eager-looking participants. He could almost feel what he called "an electric charge" in the air. A phenomena Leiv occasionally sensed in his courtroom. Something else he and Curtis had discussed back then. From Curtis's perspective, he bemoaned his lack of ability to capture each trial's particular energy. Some trials more than others, but Curtis would still complain there was often a palpable "feeling" that defied pencil and paper capture.

Then in a sudden and sidebar reflection, Leiv wondered why—in addition to dwelling so much in the past this morning— he was also being so fanciful and loose in all his thinking. Indeed, he felt the urge to shake his head, as if he could rebalance his brain activity. He didn't.

The memory excursions he blamed on Winston. The fancifulness though, Leiv ended up shrugging off, deciding— *what the hell*. He promised Lloyd he would not only be here, but also to stay for the whole shindig. Not a promise he intended to renegue on, but figured his mind was consequently making it a game of sorts to help him through what could end up a tedious morning.

Still, he certainly didn't think of himself as silly man by nature—*though Melissa definitely had thought me romantic. But other than that....* Consequently, this morning's mental flights of fancy were indeed questions for Leiv to ponder.

Such as—why look for a hidey hole in the first place, then imagine what a man he never met before would look like naked in his nudist world, then dredging up a singing defendant from a rather bizarre past trial, then latching on to the pronouncements of a reporter-artist—and now, acting like an early 1900's fiction storyteller in assessing Shiné community meeting attendees as if they were novel characters.

Yet, his seated place at the elongated table—*certainly orchestrated by Lloyd*—was perfect for doing just that. Looking around and assessing.

Lloyd had forced him out of his hidey-hole, and Leiv found himself sitting at the corner spot the farthest from the door-end of a two-table arrangement. The setup was aiming for accommodation for a large group with two long banquet-type tables lined up end-to-end. Clearly needed for the large number of attendees continuing to arrive. At first, the community meeting room felt spacious, now it seemed packed.

Who are all these people, a little voice in Leiv's head questioned yet again—this time even more insistent.

There were some Shiné residents besides Walker Johns and Jasmine Fabero he did know—like Chef-Jack, Douglas "Hermit" Chan, Mary Jones, Doc Will Walker, Margaret Deers, and Elizabeth-May to name a few—and even though he now couldn't readily find them all—Leiv supposed that like himself, they were now all sitting around the table somewhere. *Something* was up and changing around him, and he didn't yet know what. Right here in LC's isolated little Shiné.

It didn't take long before Lloyd gaveled the meeting to order. Leiv didn't miss the significance his friend was sitting at the head of the long two-table length with a big old-fashioned gavel at the ready for him. He was sure Lloyd could see everyone as they came in and was noting where they sat in his table-tableau.

Leiv's intuition also told him, his friend had not only maneuvered him into his particular seat—his right-hand-man so to speak, "shotgun" as Glover would probably dub his spot—but had also directed the Community Center meeting room setup in total. From layout to seating, and to his advantage, of course—causing Leiv to smile in appreciation at the pastor's "congregational savvy."

As the committee secretary read the minutes from the last meeting, quite loudly and succinctly Leiv thought, he heard Lloyd whispering to him—the pastor's head slightly turned toward him, and his lips barely moving behind a hand covering his mouth, "I think everyone here pretty much knows who you are by now."

Leiv nodded, surreptitiously bringing his own hand to his forehead to cover his own head movement. *Now I'm acting like a secret agent. Good grief.*

"So I don't think I need to introduce you or tell anyone yet you have to sign off. That can come later."

"Sign off what?" Leiv whispered back while moving his hand down to cover his mouth like the pastor.

Lloyd turned to Leiv directly and bestowed on him such an incredulous look, Leiv was momentarily taken aback. Next his friend did a pastoral-like rolling of his eyes and humphed under his breath without moving his lips or chest. Then Lloyd turned his attention back to the folks lining the table in front of him—seemingly dismissing Leiv's question as just plain unbelievable.

Leiv did vaguely remember some withdrawing room discussion last night about the county asking for development input from communities around the very large county. But now, he couldn't quite remember. *What's wrong with my head?*

Leiv tsked Glover-style, at himself. But instead of wasting further mental energy in self-chastisement, he went back to taking in the room and table—reminding himself to keep in mind Curtis's methods of picking out prominent traits, and noticing mannerisms for his caricatures. Of course he wasn't preparing to sketch anyone, but Leiv thought in using the artist's methods he might get a clue to *who* all these strangers were, and *what* they were about.

These assessments were not an activity Leiv would actually call fun, but something to keep him occupied until "new business" came up on the committee's agenda. At which time he would hopefully find out what was actually going on. *Should have listened better last night.*

Then for a few seconds, he felt a bit dizzy—but it passed quickly. He guessed Lloyd also mentioned this morning's agenda last night, but once again Leiv found himself wanting. This time, he sighed very slightly, almost inaudible, and hopefully not even moving his lips. He certainly didn't want Lloyd, or Adeleine sitting to his right, to know what he was feeling.

The committee secretary droned on in minute detail. He tried to listen. Rectify last night. But Leiv just couldn't focus his mind on what she was saying. Indeed, now that he really thought about it, ever since breakfast with Adeleine, he just didn't seem to be the person he knew as himself.

At the other end of the long double-table and directly facing Lloyd was Tim Teague, Jasmine's husband; with Jasmine sitting to Tim's right at a ninety degree angle like he and Lloyd. Jasmine's ordinarily rather pretty and upbeat face, from what he could see, looked strained with worry. Leiv guessed at her thoughts—*anxious about her father's survival*. Yet, she came to support her husband at this meeting. *Divided loyalties maybe?*

Leiv could now see clearly Tim had a long face with a stiffly angular jaw line and squinty eyes. Unkindly, Leiv wondered what Jasmine had seen in him—if looks had been an attraction criteria. Immediately, Leiv felt shallow—and wondered again at his silliness this morning. He cleared his throat, reminded himself of his age. Nonetheless, and mocking his introspection, he once again thought about Tim's nudist calling, and had to quickly move his eyes and mind onto the next interesting face along the long side of the table facing him.

The woman sitting next to Jasmine, was wearing a stylish business suit—he guessed from the jacket and blouse he could see. *Not the norm for Shiné.* He put her in his "business woman" people box. Though she did remind him somehow—and in a very small way—of a particular prosecuting attorney he once liked. Maybe even fancied before he met Melissa. Was it the slight amusement he saw in the corners of her mouth, despite her no-nonsense posture and tilt of her head? He expected she might even be wearing nylons and heels underneath the table.

"What are you doing?" Adeleine asked in a normal volume and tone of voice, and once again catching him off guard. Evidently only he and Lloyd saw the need for secret-agent-like communication.

"Ah...." He stammered, then was instantly irritated with himself. "Lost in the past again," he admitted.

"It's me and Father that's done that. Taken some part of your mind back to Illinois."

"You really are intuitive...and sharp." He felt himself staring at her face. *Plain, but interesting. Wonder what Curtis would say and draw?*

"Can I have that in writing?" Adeleine smiled, then made a wry face. "Not that sharp. I'm out of a job, you know. Quit before I left Springfield. And without the standard and courteous two-week notice." She shook her head. "Regret that."

"Life and circumstances can change sometimes...with just a blink it seems—" Leiv stopped himself in time before his mind and emotions revisited Melissa and the night she died on the Congress Expressway. For a few seconds, it seemed harder than usual not to let his grief take over—but he managed it.

Diverting his thoughts, he told Adeleine about Josh and Curtis, knowing she had visited his courtroom occasionally way-back-when. Leiv finished up by coming around to current circumstances—bemoaning not knowing what was going on this morning.

She listened with seeming interest and appreciation, then nodded her head when he finished, as if she agreed with Curtis's techniques for capturing and communicating a persona. Leiv wasn't sure what she thought of Josh—and she didn't enlighten him there. But she did offer in line with people assessments, "You know, I talked to Tim a bit. Not in depth, but enough to know why he's here."

"And that is?"

"He's here to pitch one of the projects that someone named Margaret is writing up. His is a Shiné nudist-sanctuary. At least that's what he called it."

"Margaret Deers is involved?"

"Who is she?"

He reminded Adeleine of the lady sitting next to her on the loveseat last night.

"Oh, yes. That very nice lady." Adeleine started a motion that looked like she was going to slap her forehead with the palm of her hand, but caught herself before she did. "And you just said I was 'sharp.' Ha!"

"Did you pick up last night she's the Chief of Police's mother?"

"The man to your right you kept whispering to?"

Leiv nodded, then Leiv almost confided further— explaining about Margaret's dalliance with his father before he married his mother. He caught himself in time. *A really bad idea.* Further, he also chastised himself again, *I've really gone loony this morning.*

"Is he here this morning?"

Leiv made a disparaging sound. "No, he's got better things to do this morning." He recalled their conversation late last night. *And where the heck is he right now?*

"Like what?" Adeleine asked.

"Like sorting out a dead body." He didn't add the unsubstantiated bits about a hired killer. Too close to home.

"Well the Margaret that was sitting next to me last night is here this morning. Further down the table on my right." She smiled wryly. "You'd have to lean forward a bit to see her."

Leiv and Adeleine both fell silent for a moment. *A comfortable silence* he thought.

Eventually Adeleine cleared her throat lightly, and inclined her head toward the other side of the table. "The lady next to the Tim guy, that's the daughter of the man who almost died yesterday, right?"

"Yes." Leiv took a long deep breath. "Sure hope he doesn't die today."

"Has he been your neighbor for long?"

"Neighbor?" It caught him as an odd term for folks spread out on such big parcels from each other. Shiné was a long way from southern California suburbia-sprawl.

Evidently trying to interpret his quizzical look, she elaborated with a question, "Wasn't the fire just across the road from you?"

He nodded. "Let's stop by there on our way home. I haven't really looked at it. Since the fire." Indeed, he'd purposefully averted his eyes coming out of Rhodes Castle driveway and making the turn to go into town earlier.

The minutes reading continued—lengthy it turned out, and informative Leiv presumed. Yet he continued to not listen. Instead, he took in the man sitting next to the lady in the business suit. Another stranger to Leiv. The man's face was large, with big eyes surrounded by webs of wrinkles encompassing deep eye sockets, while the rest of the skin on his face was smooth. Leiv couldn't see his hands, evidently the man had them clasped in his lap. He was also bald, with a developing double chin hanging below a big mouth with full lips. Face and features, all sitting firmly on a thick short neck attached to the broad shoulders of a heavy-set torso.

A perfect face for Curtis to caricature.

Besides wondering who he was, Leiv also tried to mentally draw the sketch Curtis might make of this stranger. Leiv felt his eyelids blink, and wondered why he noticed them doing so. *Autonomic reflex, right?* So, why had he noticed his own eyes blinking?

Before he could further think about his eyelids, someone down his side of the table stood up abruptly, threw a folder of loose papers across the table at the wrinkly-eye-socket man, and yelled in an angry voice, "And it's all lies!" The outraged accuser sounded like a man, and for a micro-second, Leiv felt the urge to reach for his gavel. *Quiet in the courtroom.*

Then, quite surprisingly, when leaning forward a bit to look down his side of the table to catch sight of who was making the stink, he also saw Tim Teague at the end of the table stifle a smirk. Or was it a smile? Leiv wasn't sure.

Leiv did know for certain, though, in that blink of an eyelid, his perception of the real world was definitely different this morning in Shiné Community Church.

Glover's campaign hat was stowed safely atop the file cabinet closest to his desk; while he stood to the left side of the bench that spanned part of his Shiné storefront office window, legs slightly spread, and in a fresh-from-the-cleaners dark navy-blue uniform. He was holding a mug of newly brewed coffee in his hand, looking outward. Thinking.

Among his other early morning musings, he inexplicably found himself returning several times to wondering if he made the right decision. *Taking this Shiné posting.* Then the follow-on question, *should I stay?* Characteristically, his "everyman" face revealed little of these inner thoughts.

Like Leiv, Glover also enjoyed Shiné mornings. But unlike his half-brother, it wasn't so much the visual of Shiné's eastern horizon, the sunrise colors, or the philosophical promise of a new day. *No,* it was the quiet time he liked.

Shiné's Main Street was never a hub of activity; but the early morning hours, before any shop keepers opened their doors were special—*when I'm able to enjoy them.* Especially on Sunday mornings, with fewer and later opening times—these moments were priceless for him. *Yes,* even now, rather late into the morning, it was quiet still—with most folks off at the community meeting.

Directly across the street was now a bookstore. *At last,* an actual business to catch his attention, instead of the interest-less "available for lease" sign hanging crookedly in its front window for so long. The new leasee, a writer—a nice man by Glover's first assessment—was living in back of his store, and probably contrary to county guidelines. Glover hadn't checked. Didn't care. Though he did have Walker surreptitiously check for safety concerns.

This morning, Glover thought he caught a flicker of light in the back recesses of the store. He smiled, thinking the man — *Nate was it?* — must really like books to want to wake up every morning surrounded by them.

His undirected thoughts moved from Nate and his books, to Leiv's words from last night. "You know there are five." Glover's smile widened in recalling Leiv's "revelation" about the Mojave Stones. Leiv had seemed so worried, then relieved. Funny, in that he had already guessed at such a scenario when he retrieved the stone on the ground in front of Elizabeth-May's burnt out chimney last spring. The now polished gem continued to sit in his top desk drawer where he had left it. Sort of like it was his connection to his grandfather LC from way back when the old coot gave several to his friend Jules for his chimney. Glover didn't think of himself as particularly sentimental in that area. *But still.*

He sighed, and forced his gaze left, to the north, toward Shiné's Community Church. As he suspected, the parking lot was much fuller than usual. Earlier, only his mother's and Lloyd's cars were there. To set up the meeting room, she'd informed him last night. *I really should go down there.*

He sighed again, but didn't move.

No, he wanted to stay right where he was, mulling over his thoughts about the Noiseless Killer, and what he'd heard just this morning about this hit man.

Our earlier speculation was correct. He'd barely arrived in his office a couple hours earlier when the phone had rung. Needles Deputy Sheriff Brad Temper.

"Someone *has* taken the Noiseless killer out." Even over the phone Glover caught a touch of excitement in the Deputy's voice. "That's the word here in Needles. Comes from scuttle-butt from Las Vegas — whatever the hell that means." He laughed and Glover laughed with him.

"The birthmark?"

"Yep, came through already. The body we've got is this Noiseless guy."

"So, the body is yours now?"

Glover heard a muffled chuckle from Brad's end. "Yep, you've done your duty as far as Officer Bellaeu and CHP are concerned."

"That's good—"

Brad cut him off. "But there's more, Chief Deers. You know your idea there was a vigilante killer out there?"

Glover nodded as if Brad could see him.

"Well," Brad continued. "You're not alone. Added scuttle-butt—but this time, tri-state, California, Arizona, and Nevada. That's who they think took Noiseless out. They've kept the vigilante angle out of the news so far. But it's the talk, I'm told, around all police stations concerned."

Glover heard Brad take a deep breath, "And there's more…"

"Go on," Glover encouraged.

"Illinois state police also think there's another one—"

"Another what?" Glover felt his body tense.

"Hit man. 'The Fixer' they're calling him. From Chicago."

Almost immediately after Glover disconnected, Deputy Tanya Lewis called.

"Talked to my contact Sheriff's Deputy friend in Sangamon County, Illinois. She couldn't tell me outright, but definitely hinted heavily there's a threat against a prominent politician and his daughter."

"'Threat' as in a contract hit?"

"Yep."

"Hardly believable…"

"Yep."

After Tanya rang off, he'd sat for awhile. Thinking some more.

"I should go down to the church," he told his empty office. But he had a disturbing inkling of an idea.

Consequently, Glover had next gone over to his window looking out to Main Street—where he now stood—further indulging his speculative thoughts. He definitely was not in a hurry to leave yet. His mother, Leiv, Lloyd...*they can all take care of themselves and protect that Adeleine person.* Besides, *What could possibly go wrong in a church community meeting?*

Where the heck is Glover? Leiv figured he could have pulled away by now—*for awhile at least.* He also expected since the Chief of Police's mother, Margaret, was here—he would eventually be, too. Not that he wanted to go as far as calling Glover on the phone—figuring he might actually be still busy with the funny-named hit man info-gathering.

Nonetheless, here, right now, "things" were getting a little out of hand when people started throwing papers and yelling at each other. The voice in his head was petulant, accusatory, causing Leiv to again admonish himself for all his adolescent and fanciful thoughts this morning. *I haven't taken my vitamins for the day yet,* so he figured nothing chemical should be happening. And he'd cooked breakfast himself—*nothing strange there.*

Fortunately, the folder-tossing man sat back down with a humph loud enough to be heard around the room, and Pastor Lloyd Apply quickly stood and made a few pastor-like, but pointed admonishments. No one else said anything—in fact, a hush fell over the room. Hopefully, from here on, the meeting would continue in a civil fashion. Just the same, "Glover should be here," Leiv murmured. *To keep the peace.*

"Who?" Adeleine asked in a low and covert-like voice.

"Glover."

Leiv leaned forward a bit more to get a better look at the folder-throwing buffoon, and to see who else might be in attendance. Known acquaintances, and strangers he hoped to continue fancifully characterize—again using Curtis's methods. Stretching as far as he could to look down the table to his right, Leiv immediately caught sight of Hermit Chan sitting to the left of the folder thrower. Leiv learned when the moving making crew was around last spring, Douglas Chan was called "Hermit" for a reason. *And* recluses don't come to committee meetings, *do they?* Although, Hermit was getting a little more sociable. *He came to my Saturday night to-do, didn't he?*

Hermit caught his glance and winked. Leiv definitely liked Hermit, and smiled his way with an accompanying tip of the head. Leiv felt himself relax a bit—with the unidentified strangeness he was feeling diminishing somewhat. *Funny that,* a friendly wink from Hermit Chan being a calming force. Leiv still, once again chastised himself for not knowing what was going on—and he guessed, *whatever* was going on was not something he was either anticipating, or prepared to handle.

The meeting resumed and the stalwart minute-reader finally finished her task.

After Margaret Deers next read the mailed-in proposals Lloyd suggested a short "potty-break" In agreement with the pastor's suggestion, he noticed several heads bob and relieved facial expressions.

So many strangers. Though there were several friends in attendance, too. Taking a count without being too obvious, Leiv also formally placed in his seating arrangement Walker Johns, Elizabeth-May, Mary Jones, Doc Will Walker, and even Chef Jack. Seeing them all seated in the room, he felt himself relax a tad more, and thought, *I can get through this meeting.* Nonetheless, he was still concerned about where the stalwart judge-person he used to be—*until sometime this morning*—had disappeared to.

With purpose, Leiv brought his attention back to going around the table. Indeed, he had survived many a seemingly endless meeting back in his courtroom days, and reaffirmed he would make it through this Sunday morning—and to that end,

Leiv continued with his Curtis-like assessments while Margaret read proposals, and on through the restroom break.

Next to the wrinkly-eyed man was another woman, whose eyes—in contrast to said man—were attractive and intelligent. Unfortunately, he thought her pinched nose and lips conjured up a slightly dour countenance accentuated by a long face, and a tight-set and thin mouth line. Disconcertingly offsetting her no-nonsense facial aspect, was a wide streak of white hair sweeping from her forehead and backward through a sea of beauty-salon coiffured red hair. Her hands were clasped primly on the table in front of her—and Leiv wondered if her feet were crossed in a matronly-like manner under the table—*or?* She didn't get up when the opportunity was offered to use the restroom, causing him to squelch yet another childish urge—this time, to actually look under the table and check her feet out.

Margaret had read the written proposals from absentee contributors quickly and concisely. The ones Leiv retained memory-wise were, *an animal rescue, a second bar, a gem stone museum, a cheese shop, a newspaper, a writer's retreat, and of all things, a winery specializing in Mojave Desert-grown grapes.* He was surprised there were grapes being grown in desert soil at all. And he doubted Chef Jack was interested in another bar competing with TGS's.

Returning to his latest analysis of attending presenters— even though he still childishly wanted to look under the table at the crazy-hair-colored woman's feet—Leiv remained unable to snap-judge this woman. Consequently, he couldn't tuck her away into one of the personality-type boxes he'd mentally created over the years. Indeed, even with Curtis's suggestions still guiding him, no courtroom sketch easily presented itself either. *Was she an enigma?* A pleasant thought given all the "characters" parading through his courtrooms over the years; and now through his memories. *Unique—and not contrived.*

For a moment, Leiv forced his curiosity lenses back on himself, wondering what he was doing with his own feet under the table, and what they might say about him? How unique was he in the way of people populating the world? *Not very,* he bemused, then smiled to himself—returning his thoughts to feet. Funny, he could recognize "the blink of his eyes," but not know what the heck his feet were doing. Leiv knew his brain was running at a speed he wasn't used to, and going in directions uncharacteristic to his personality. *And this Curtis-like analysis of everyone...*

He saw Adeleine was watching him quite openly. She winked, and he certainly didn't know what to make of that. Definitely not the same as Hermit's wink. *Is she reading my mind?*

"Are you taking in our gathering still?" she asked, again, *sotto voce.* "Trying to figure them out? Draw a courtroom kind of sketch of each one like the guy you told me about earlier?"

"Yes," Leiv answered, concluding she was *definitely* reading his mind. *What a unique and possibly strange young woman.* He felt he might have made a shoulder-shiver kind of movement, but doubted he actually had. Then the answer came to him at last why he was acting and thinking so strangely. *Hester's tea for sure.*

Adeleine got up. "I'm going to the restroom." She pointed to the door next to his earlier hidey-hole behind them. "In back of us, in the kitchen. I should have gone when your pastor first suggested. Now there's a line."

Leiv nodded, and though remaining seated, he followed her with his eyes. In that moment, and in another blink-of-the-eye, Leiv internalized the responsibility Winston had dumped on him. Like it or not, resenting his highhandedness or not—for the nonce, he was Adeleine's caretaker, and he needed to start acting like one. *Hester's tea be damned.*

The aroma of hot chocolate and freshly brewed coffee had not only filled the kitchen, but proceeded to waft its way in and engulf the meeting room with two distinct and wonderful aromas. Leiv liked them both, and though he didn't go get a refill, he did take in the chocolate and coffee produced ambiance. And once Adeleine returned safely—he also tried adjusting his attitude to a responsible community member. Reminding himself, in this "arena" he was representing LC, whether he wanted to or not.

Even though a full half-hour passed before everyone was again seated, and refreshment refills grabbed, Leiv thought the time went by rather fast. And pleasantly with Adeleine to chat with some of the time and "assessments" to make. Especially since Lloyd was off "mingling" as a good pastor should.

When everyone was again seated and ready to conduct current business, his body clock told Leiv morning had morphed into afternoon. He seldom wore a watch, and since all were again seated, he didn't want to turn around and blatantly look backwards up at the schoolhouse clock hanging on the wall behind him to know for certain. His hidey-hole was right below the clock—and it was beginning to feel like an eternity since he stood there with his friend Lloyd—taking in Shiné Community Church's meeting room. *What a morning,* he now thought.

After everyone was settled, Margaret brought over and handed Lloyd a folder with what looked liked several sheets of paper peeking out. She also whispered a few words in the pastor's ear.

Leiv stifled an unbidden and surprising yawn. *Not now,* he admonished his brain and body. *Maybe I should have had some coffee.* To counteract his sudden sleepiness, he tried to imagine the beautiful and crisp fall day he knew awaited him outside. Fresh invigorating air. Maybe the fall imagery would wake him up and clear his head. *Almost the beginning of my fourth year in Shiné,* Leiv further mused—and he knew for sure fall was becoming his favorite season. Indeed, he had arrived in Shiné three falls earlier.

And what a three years it's been.

"Mister Keith Meldon," Lloyd called out.

Leiv presumed Keith Meldon was the first name on the piece of paper he could see now sitting on the table in front of Lloyd. *Why can't I pay attention.*

"You're up first with your proposition," Lloyd said loudly.

Proposition for what? Though by now, Leiv knew what was going on. He just didn't want to accept the reality the county was hitting up Margaret Deers with input for "enhancing" Shiné. Nor did he want to remember the details of the whole awful happening. He rubbed his forehead.

Obviously this meeting was to gather enhancement-input. Of course, anything like that would end up involving him, and maybe Glover. Yet again, he beat himself up for not listening last night and giving Lloyd a piece of his mind earlier. *As if I could ever really get mad at Lloyd.*

What a god-awful headache and mess this is going to be, Leiv almost said aloud. He must have sighed or made some kind of disparaging noise, because Lloyd turned his head enough to give him an ugly look. Not that the pastor's looks could actually be called "ugly." Disapproving was more accurate.

Imagining the fall day *outside* was not working to relax him *inside.* Just the opposite. Leiv now very much wanted to escape—rush into that crisp fall air he imagined was waiting for him. He looked up at the row of light-emitting rectangular windows high on the wall above the row of seating along the wall. *Fall awaits out there.*

In the chairs below the window, Margaret Deers was ensconced in the middle seat, and was looking down at some more papers in her lap. He could neither read her face, nor tell anything about outside through the windows above her. Though Leiv, now way, way, out of his character boundaries, fancied he thought he saw an Athol branch brush the window directly above Margaret—with a magical looking bird flying off it. Then he heard what he thought was the whistling sound of wind. Leiv knew it was all in his imagination. Brain circuits going totally bananas. *Will this Hester tea ever quit?*

The man with the wrinkly eyes—evidently he was Keith Meldon—cleared his throat, looked around as if to ensure he had everyone's attention, and then started in to what Leiv thought after several minutes of listening—one of the most ego-stroking *curriculum vitae* he'd heard since pre-trial presentations in his chambers. He also remembered expert-witnesses who would go on endlessly. Then there were the law clerk interviews....

However, the increased volume and emphasis in Meldon's voice, surprisingly high and squeaky for such a pompous man, brought Leiv back to current events. He needed to listen. Keith Meldon had finally gotten to his actual proposal. The wrinkly-eyed man wanted a re-enactment center. Right in the heart of Shiné—or somewhere slightly south of town, but before reaching the land Lucca was caretaking.

Where his double-wide burned down...and a good man now lies in intensive care at the hospital.

If Leiv understood Keith Meldon correctly, there would also be a yearly festival—with costumes—showing how life was for the early Route 66 trail blazers through the years. Dwelling on the old ways of doing things. It would be a living museum, sort of, with re-enactments of Route 66 early homesteading. *Like digging septic pits,* Leiv mentally scoffed, *without instructional aide from the internet.*

Counteracting his reactionary negative thoughts, Leiv heard, "Sounds like fun," from someone on his side of the long table. Hermit? He didn't think so, and started to move forward a little to look, but felt a bit dizzy and quickly pulled back seeking the rigidity and bracing stiffness of his chair back.

Meldon's final proposal point was—there were a lot of foreign travelers, European and Asian "doing The Route." He believed said travelers would love seeing a piece of the American experience in action. Then finally, after talking far too long on his proposal, Meldon finished drawing his word-pictures of his Route 66 village-park.

After Meldon, without another break, and after quickly consulting the list in front of him, Lloyd said, "Mister Nathan Johnson, you're next, the floor is yours. But please, no more outbursts, physical or verbal."

The man who had thrown the folder across the table at Meldon stood up quickly and sighed heavily. His body language and tone reeked with condescension and arrogance. "Shiné needs culture, not a tacky olden-days amusement park," he said. "Nothing amusing about all the work you had to do back then. The world has changed. What we need, is to bring art and culture to this part of the Mojave. My proposal is for an Art Park with inside and outside sculptures, paintings—including experimental pieces—"

Is he the guy who opened the bookstore on main? Leiv asked himself, then tried to remember, but wasn't sure. He'd only met him once.

Without standing, the woman with the white streak and unknown feet position interrupted Johnston with a strong, firm, and resounding voice. "What will bring culture to Shiné is a theatre building. We have plenty of budding young actors in the area. And not just from the Junior colleges east and west of here."

Leiv guessed she was a teacher after hearing her speak and her concern for young people. *Which he didn't think Shiné had many of. Or do we?*

"Adele," Nathan Johnson said, coming back at her in an equally insistent tone. "A theatre only benefits a handful of actors, while my Art Park—"

"Benefits you." She made several sounds through her teeth that gave the undeniable impression she thought Johnson was scum-of-the-earth. "Who do you think cares about East Coast snobbish junk being fobbed off as art?" Still she sat. Hands crossed at the wrist on the table.

Leiv tried again to lean forward, this time successful, and saw Nathan's body was taut, and the cheek on the side of his face Leiv could see, was actually puffing in and out. He wished for a Curtis substitute who could sketch the enraged caricature Johnson brought to mind.

Adeleine whispered, "Wow, Judge, this is getting exciting. Who would have thought, out here in a church no less?"

Her comment sent his mind back in time again, this time to several almost-brawls in his courtroom. Leiv smiled slightly, remembering the incidents.

Once again, Adeleine echoed his thoughts. "Reminds me of some of the brouhahas in your courtroom."

Pastor Lloyd Apply, well mannered and controlled as he usually was, said in the firmest voice Leiv had ever heard him use, "Sit down, Mr. Johnson. And you do not have the floor, Ms. Mason."

Leiv mentally abandoned his Curtis exercise. *Can't possibly cartoon Meldon.*

Slowly, but eventually, Lloyd continued and finished his list. A representative from a known hotel chain wanted to have permitted an additional motel for his chain. Another representative from a well known fast food chain had the same goal.

Another man with an extremely long beard Leiv had heretofore not noticed, wanted to build earthen-housing for a desert monastery. And a woman in the back corner at the other end of the table in a long robe claimed she had evidence Shiné was at the end of an ancient Celtic-site. *Something about ley lines?* Leiv almost laughed aloud. He did hear Adeleine snigger—but managed to ignore her. Then, to his great surprise and wonderment, even Hermit had a turn. *Why would a recluse want to bring more people to Shiné?*

Hermit's enigmatic input was for a bell tower. Hermit didn't say what kind exactly—recorded, real? A tall bell tower-like structure? Or a small bell holder out front? Or where? Leiv was left totally confused. And somewhere in his bell tower cats were involved. Leiv guessed he wanted the tower attached to Shiné Community Church where they were now sitting? Leiv did find Hermit's information about the number of active bell-ringing churches in the country interesting, and he made a mental note he wanted to find out more.

Next to him, he felt Lloyd straighten his shoulders—and looking more directly at him, Leiv could see from Lloyd's posture, even he was wearing out. "I want to thank everyone for coming in this morning," Lloyd said. "Mrs. Deers," he gave a recognition-nod in Margaret direction, "will be taking all your input into account, and writing it up in the form required by the county—"

He was interrupted by Tim Teague at the other end of the table clearing his throat loudly, then proclaiming in a neutral fashion, "You've seem to have forgotten me." He smiled. "You didn't call on me, Pastor."

Lloyd looked down at his sheet, "Oh my, yes you're right Tim." He paused as if reading for a moment or two, then said "Oh my," again—but with a different inference. He cleared his throat, swallowed hard, and said, "My apologies, the floor is yours Mr. Teague."

As it turned out, Tim Teague wanted to set up a nudist ranch in Shiné. Another one in addition to the two his father had already established. As Jasmine's husband stood up to explain his proposal, Leiv once again was forced to cover his mouth to keep from smiling. *Something, perverse I know, in wanting to picture Tim naked again*—but this time he was wearing a chef's apron and sporting a *toque blanche* atop his head.

Barely audible even to himself, Leiv murmured, "I know I've been drugged." How else to explain all this morning's out of character flights-of-fancy. *The hot chocolate?* No, everyone was drinking from carafes filled from the same large commercial pot.

Hester's tea. No way to get around it.

Tim had gone on for quite awhile, "We need a nudist colony. Nudists of the world are crying out for more places to go. The desert is the perfect spot."

But a chain?

As Leiv's mind kept bouncing around uninhibited, his thoughts next landed on Shiné's former mayor, Tucker Oakes. And his murdering wife, Ida. After Ida went to jail and Tucker took leave, Shiné had gone on without a mayor. Leiv considered that maybe it was high time they elected another one? He wondered how that mayoral-process had worked in the past—he wasn't in Shiné at the time. *Yes,* Shiné needed a new mayor, and he needed to ask Glover how to get that done.

And where was Glover anyway?

Then like a genie rubbing a mental lantern, Leiv saw Glover leaning against the frame of the meeting room entry door. Hat in hands in front of him, head dipped to conceal his features. *Holding back a grin*—Leiv was sure. And possibly taking in who was present. He turned his eyes away quickly, didn't want Glover to notice *him* noticing *him*.

After breakfast, Mugs picked up his gun in Baker—delivered there by a well-paid and friendly dealer from Nevada. But his compact Bushnell binoculars, he'd brought with him from Chicago. Both were at hand now as Mugs sat in hiding near the property where his target was supposed to be staying.

He needed to scope out the lay of the land in order to get just the right shot—and Mugs prided himself on being well organized and meticulous in scouting-out and planning his fixes. Further to achieve that end, he also had several types of paper maps sitting on his rental's console next to him. Strategically placed on a ledge-like protrusion underneath the touch-screen apparatus, which was providing an unintended physical table for his printed maps. Even though his rental car agent proudly explained this console screen section had an app, with the latest bells and whistles when it came to GPS, Mugs held his tongue and refrained from explaining he wasn't about to rely on computer apps and programs when it came to "fixing."

Besides, he was a professional, *always careful* — leave no trail of where, why, and when. Especially nowadays with, *what did they call it?* The words came to him, "Electronic footprint stuff." He shook his head. "And as if a GPS would know about all the unmapped dirt roads in this damn desert."

Silly for a man like him, Mugs knew, but he couldn't get himself past there being something spooky about the Mojave. Things didn't seem to work exactly like they did in Chicago — or anyplace else he'd been on a "fix."

Unconsciously, he rolled his shoulders like a prize fighter getting ready for battle.

Parked as he was at his first destination point, he was also taking a few minutes to think — before doing the deed. Making sure he didn't need to modify or expand his plan. Completing this job was close at hand, and Mugs could taste his excitement building. Of course, every event was always laced with some apprehension. *But that was part of the excitement, now wasn't it?*

Then at the end, there was the joy of a job well done. *Or there used to be.* The thought surprised him, and he wasn't sure why and where it came from. Mugs uncharacteristically sighed.

He had driven down to Shiné from the north this time, taking the I-15 exit near Baker that barely marked Shiné's existence with a minor-league-sized sign — in faded small white letters, and easily missed. He was traveling at slow traffic-flow speed at the time, and figured if he hadn't been prepared like he always was, he might have missed the sign completely. Mugs physically patted the map stack on his console, then mentally patted himself on the back.

Out of nowhere, a gust of wind found his parking hideaway, and hit the side of his little white rental hard enough for him to feel it — then complain again, "Damn desert."

The wind reminded Mugs, he had been on this road before, and experienced Mojave wind gusts before when he arrived from the South. Nonetheless, and even though he was approaching Shiné from a different direction—more unpleasant memories also intruded on his thoughts.

Sand dunes, car chases, dead bodies in cellars, Anthony L's ditsy wife... "Things" did eventually get taken care of—Fixer results accomplished—*and* without having to kill a woman. Or anyone, for that matter.

"Funny that," he mumbled, remembering. Mugs even had luck on the Mojave wind front—what with gusts blowing Anthony L's damn notebook away. "And I got out of this desert okay." *Can't catch The Fixer that easy now, can they?*

Mugs Nightshade felt quite comfortable musing and talking to himself within his rental car's safe cocoon. No one was around. *Unbelievable that damn wind was able to find me.* He was parked on the side of the road, not quite completely hidden, but definitely surrounded by a sizable and camouflaging outgrowth of mature Athols. For reconnoitering purposes, Mugs figured he was effectively tucked away in this little tree-pocket at the base of the turn off going up to the fancy castle-house to his right.

To his left looked like the remnants of a really bad fire—burnt trees, soot-encrusted sand, and to the back—maybe the shell of a house? A mobile maybe? He wasn't sure. *If I can lure her over there....* And only one county-type truck left on the scene, and he doubted very much he'd be seen. Or would be seen at night.

Well, he planned to scope everything out before making his move. Including sneaking up to the castle-like house up the hill under cover of darkness tonight.

"A castle in the desert," he scoffed.

In the meantime, he considered checking out the fire site. Just a curious spectator if the lone fireman saw him. *Got plenty of time to kill.* He didn't like *stuff* like that—*unexpected stuff*—he couldn't explain.

Like the dead body in the root cellar last spring. For a second he wondered if the Noiseless Killer started the fire he was now looking at? But that didn't make any sense. If he'd taken her out in that fire, Noiseless would have reported back to their employer. Maybe even sent a proof of death picture on his cell phone. Besides, the story he got was the woman was still alive and would be with that man who lived in the castle place. Why else would he need to scare her? Silly woman should have arrived last week if she flew. "How else do you get out to this damn desert?"

Mugs scoffed and realized he kind of liked talking to himself aloud. He was a good audience. Next, he considered, "Maybe the fire was a diversion?" *Nah.*

Finally, not being able to make anything else fit the scenario he was looking at, Mugs decided the fire must have been an accident and unrelated.

Then, seemingly out of nowhere, and hitting him squarely in his gut, Mugs "felt" the Noiseless Killer was dead. Somebody had killed him. He didn't really "know" he was dead, but intuitively *felt* it. *But who would kill him?* He hadn't heard any word on Noiseless being a marked man.

"Nothing in this damn desert ever makes sense."

Another blast of wind hit his car, this time from the back—and when he looked to his rear view mirror, Mugs saw what looked like a ball of rolling sand running down the roadway. His little car was evidently in the mass's side wind. He watched until whatever it was passed his tree clump and moved on south toward I-40. Whatever he witnessed wasn't large enough to call a sandstorm, but definitely bigger then one of those foot-level dust-bally things, or tumbleweed-bally-things he'd seen before.

This time in response to the sand-ball and his thoughts, Mugs involuntarily shivered as if to shake it all off.

Fortunately his windows were up—*learned that last time*—and his vents closed—yet the air smelled different? Not dusty, but he wasn't sure exactly how to identify how the air had changed. *Dirt doesn't smell*, he was sure. "At least not in Chicago." *Or did it?*

Then Mugs remembered—with a fondness he would never lose—his grandmother and her house on Paulina Street. Him a kid still, *such a long time ago*. Besides the Nightshade she grew along her alley fence, there was her humongous vegetable garden. *Took up half the yard.*

And she had talked to him—an eager and willing-to-listen little kid—about the soil smelling sweet. And knowing by the odor what she needed to do soil wise. "But that was black soil. Real dirt. Not like the stuff out here." Mugs was sure sand didn't smell. *How could it?* It was dead soil, *now wasn't it?* Not black like in his home town.

Finally, he decided to scope the whole area out tonight—then tomorrow he would be ready to take her out. *Or maybe tonight if I get a chance.* "Get in and out of this damn desert. Quick."

A prospect which brought a smile.

Once again out of seemingly nowhere, and yet another reminder of his revulsion and inability to understand all-things-Mojave—David Milhouse popped into his brain. His cousin's son, Milhouse, a fancy LA set designer of all things, was getting married to some ditsy local broad. Going to be living out here somewhere. He was the same guy who drove to the sand dune ledge to see if there were any hunks of book lying around after the winds had done their thing. Mugs had never met the guy, probably a good thing. "I'm definitely not going to look him up."

More thoughts swirled around in the mix a good fixer like himself needed to consider to ensure success. *There was* that throwaway rumor of a rogue-cop vigilante out West. California in particular. But Mugs had a hard time imagining such a scenario and doubted the scuttlebutt was true. Not cop-like in his experience—and he moved the consideration to the back burner in his calculations.

But there was that cop in the diner Mugs was sure he'd seen before—somewhere on this trip before the diner. *Eyeing me.*

Another blast of wind hit his little white rental from the side again.

Mugs grumbled, "Damn desert."

Leiv saw everyone else was in some stage of escaping what had turned out to be a hideously long meeting. Last to leave were Margaret Deers, her son Glover, Adeleine, and himself. Indeed, rather quickly they were the only ones remaining in the room.

He empathized with the desire to get out and stretch—breathe some fresh air. Not that it was technically stuffy inside. The Shiné Community Church meeting room was roomy with good air circulation. There was also a feeling of "openness" from the large kitchen pass-through window, and its two swinging-doors. *No*, he hadn't really felt cramped. And the air was not stale.

Indeed, Lloyd had explained at one Saturday night get-together, how he had a special setting on the churches heating and cooling system that just brought in outside air. *"Like in your car."* The Pastor didn't like what he called "airplane-air" here in the meeting room, or in the church area either. *"Always kid-germs flying around,"* Lloyd had un-pastorally let slip after too much Bristol Crème.

After recalling what he knew about the room, Leiv decided what actually caused the wholesale and fast room-emptying—was the magnitude of all those "gall-darned proposals," to use Lloyd's actual words. Especially following such a long and comprehensive minute-reading.

Terry Hall—he'd eventually learned her name—was a conscientious, thorough, and dedicated church secretary—hence such complete and lengthy notes. Then on top of that, the proposals for Shiné's new development attractions had *all* been long, over explained, over footnoted, and aggrandized to the hilt.

"Well, looks like I've got my hands full," Margaret said to the three remaining of them by way of bidding her own goodbye. She re-adjusted and re-cinched her gargantuan purse hanging from her shoulder. She'd already secured her stack of manila folders, wedging and pressing them firmly against her chest, and lodged them there with her bent right forearm.

Then looking at Leiv in particular, she added, "I seem to have a knack for getting pulled into other people's games."

He wasn't sure what Margaret meant by "other people's games." He did however, make a mental note to think about her comment later. *There's something there she's trying to tell me.* But Leiv didn't know what. He did know they shared some like sensibilities—fondness for Shiné skyline views, appreciation of Shiné sunsets, and memory-connections to the past back to his father Everett, and even his grandfather LC.

Maybe she's talking about Winston and Adeleine? And a possible killer looking for them? Playing Winston's *game*—hinting the wily politician had sucked him right into his problems? Or maybe a scam of some sort? Is Margaret trying to warn me? There were many possibilities as to "other people's games" —but now was not the time to press her on the point.

Leiv was very fond of Margaret. Indeed, her pleasant and often-smiling oval face, silver hair, and sixties style attire were comforting on several levels. He had also become fond of her cats, Samara and Silky. And over the last two years, he'd come to trust her from their conversations—mainly during relaxed withdrawing room exchanges at his Saturday night get togethers. Even now, this moment, and in such different circumstances, Leiv could envision her sitting on the loveseat-styled settee— fireplace hues accentuating and warming her face as she smiled at him pleasantly. Margaret was now a mainstay in his growing Shiné family.

Sure hopes she feels the same way about me. Because— catching himself mid-thought, Leiv once again realized his mind wasn't working as it should. Here he was thinking about how much he liked Margaret, envisioning her sitting on the settee in LC's withdrawing room, smiling at him, and him feeling all family-like and gushy in return—while in reality they were standing in Shiné Church's meeting room after a long tedious meeting which could have serious implications he needed to know about. Things he should care about—because LC would care about them.

I've been unwittingly drugged by Hester. Has to be the case.

"So nice seeing you again, Mrs. Deers," he heard Adeleine saying to Margaret standing right next to her. Then Adeleine hugged Margaret as if she'd known her a lifetime.

Glover's mother reciprocated with an equally generous hug, then gave him and her son individual departing smiles, turned around, and was gone before Leiv could add anything more. Not that he yet had any clear questions he wanted to ask her. For sure, though, he needed to think a bit on the teaser she'd thrown out to him. *Other people's games.*

Adeleine next said, "She's such a nice lady." Then turning her gaze to Glover in particular, "You're lucky to have such a cool mom."

Leiv knew Adeleine's mother, Yolanda, died when she was just a teenager, and if he remembered correctly, it was breast cancer that took her. He figured Adeleine's comment had special meaning.

She turned to him. "Sorry I didn't remember her right away after just meeting her last night. I'm not used to that liquor you serve." She shook her head. "And Margaret was sitting right next to me."

Glover chuckled. "That Harvey's stuff of Leiv's is easy to go down, but comes with a wallop and brain alterations you don't feel until much later."

"Not like some teas I could mention," Leiv said. Indeed, he now felt a bit dizzy—fortunately the feeling passed quickly.

"Tea?" she asked.

Leiv proceeded to tell them his speculation about Hester's tea can, and some unknown hallucinogenic he suspected she had concocted and stored within.

"Oh no," Adeleine exclaimed—sounding to Leiv as if she were half surprised and half amused. "Glad I mainly drank coffee this morning."

Glover clicked out the side of his mouth and asked, "Think we should send some into the forensics lab?"

By way of response, Leiv made an exaggerated put-upon face accompanied with an eye roll.

Then without transition of any kind, Leiv's emotion and thoughts shifted—and he wondered for a second if he should tell Adeleine who Margaret and Glover were—relationship wise to him. *Margaret being my father's first love, and Glover my brother via my father.* In an instantaneous follow-on mental swing, Leiv emphatically admonished himself—*absolutely not.*

Then, in a third swinging whoosh of thought and emotion, he questioned why he even wanted to share such an intimate confidence with Adeleine in the first place? He barely knew her. *Tea,* he concluded. *Taking me all over the place.*

His attention eventually swung back to Glover who was now talking in an almost whispered voice—even though their little group was alone in the meeting room and standing right next to each other. "Deputy Sheriff Brad Temper got confirmation on the body in the culvert."

Leiv thought Glover's tone was unusually conspiratorial, and laced with a touch of child-like excitement. Unusual for the Chief Glover Deers he knew. He was also surprised by the information. "That was fast." Leiv almost mimicked Glover's clicking out the corner of his mouth, but again, caught himself in time. "That's an almost immediate forensic analysis. Just like on TV."

"Connections," Glover responded with what Leiv took as a forced flatness. He remembered shared prior discussions—where they had discussed and chuckled over TV forensic levities and license. Glover looked at Adeleine. "I guess I shouldn't reveal that—about the connections part. They also had some prior alerts."

She smiled. "Chief, I come from Illinois politics. Know all about connections." Her voice—almost with each word—morphed from lighthearted to more somber. Adeleine finished delivering her clearly evolving thoughts by squinting her eyes, shifting her gaze to Leiv, and adding in a decidedly more serious tone, "And that's probably the reason I'm here, Judge. Political happenings that shouldn't have occurred—or promises not kept that should have. Occurred that is."

Leiv nodded his understanding. *Yes,* Winston had probably crossed the wrong person—who had in turn complained to a connection. He doubted Winston had direct dealings with gangsters—but somebody he knew certainly might. And even though he wasn't a person to let fear easily overtake him. *Received too many threats from criminals about sentences over the years.* Still, he had felt fear just then, if only momentarily.

But for some reason, this was a different kind of fear—*yet oddly familiar.* Then he remembered. That awful day in superior court, at least five years previous—*maybe much longer now that I think about it*—mandatory security x-rays weren't in effect everyplace yet. Leiv knew his mind played regression-games with dates, times, exact facts in several other instances—happenings he didn't want to remember exactly when they happened.

That particular day back then in his courtroom—a punk had pulled out a Glock semi-automatic, jumped up on the bench he was sitting on, and holding the pistol with two hands, started waving it around in a helter-skelter way—and shouting incoherently about killing everyone over a perceived injustice to his imprisoned brother. Anyone in his courtroom could have been the punk's unlucky victim. *Dead. Yes,* it was that same fright he felt now—though to a much lesser amount, but it was the same-flavored fear Leiv experienced that day. Back then, he'd known the answer was to talk that crazed-killer down—protect everyone in his courtroom.

But this morning, right now, standing right inside the door to Shiné Community Church meeting room, in the Mojave Desert, in his grandfather's tiny legacy town of Shiné, Adeleine Moore and uniformed Glover Deers at his sides, Leigh Everett-Rhodes nonetheless not only felt scared, but he didn't have a clue as what he needed to do. Just that he needed to protect Adeleine—regardless of how the circumstances had come about bringing her here to Shiné. He didn't even know for sure "who" the enemy was. Nonetheless he reaffirmed, *my duty is clear.* Afraid, or not.

His legs felt weak, and he wanted to sit down. Not here though. *Outside in my truck.* It had turned into an extremely long day, and Leiv realized how god-awful tired he must be. But looking past Adeleine and Glover, out through the doorway connecting the community meeting room and the church proper, he saw "them" heading his way.

In seconds Leiv was back dealing with current circumstances—and with the unpleasant realization that his "day at church" was not yet over.

There were at least six of them, and their group was heading toward the meeting room door—with him, Glover, and Adeleine directly in their path. Leiv guessed they were around fifteen or sixteen in age. *Fresh faced and eager eyed,* he thought. *Makes me feel old as dirt.*

Leiv sighed loud enough for Glover to hear, who whispered in response and seemingly without moving his lips, "You know what they're called?"

Leiv managed to squeeze in another little sigh. "No. But you're going to tell me, right?"

Adeleine beat Glover to the answer, "The Caretakers. Pastor Apply told me at your soiree last night."

Soiree?

"Yeah," Glover said, agreeing—then he added insider information of his own. "They're supposed to be going around visiting the sick and infirmed, taking meals to them, picking up all the windblown trash we have around here, taking out inside trash, keeping them company…good works kind of thing. They even have a mission statement."

"How come I don't know anything about them?"

"Because they came to my office specifically to see if there was something I wanted done."

Teenage deputy wannabes?

"And," Lloyd said, appearing from nowhere and now standing right behind them—his voice quite emphatic and rather loud Leiv thought. "You don't know about The Caretakers because you don't come to church, Leiv." His friend had snuck in behind them from the kitchen, and looked far more pleased with himself than a pastor should. *Rather smug, actually.*

Engaging in their little *tête-à-tête* meant he and Adeleine would not escape the group of young people descending upon them. Glover looked like he didn't care.

But teenagers were not Leiv's forte. Melissa though, he remembered fondly, had enough empathy and understanding of the younger generations for the both of them. *Thank goodness.* He had seen far too many gang members, their victims, and disappointed parents in his courtroom. Probably unfairly skewed his viewpoint—but there it was.

Leiv felt a quick little unintended jerk of his head. *Darned tea again,* he guessed was still making his mind jump all over his past life, and evidently causing some unwanted physical reactions along with the memories. He almost bemoaned aloud, *good grief,* but yet again caught himself. He managed to dredge up one of his stock professional noncommittal-expressions to plaster across his face. He thought maybe seeing Glover in uniform would cause the teenagers to move quickly into the meeting room—having a sobering kind of effect even though they'd already met him. Then he and Adeleine could make a quick getaway.

He was wrong.

Once barely inside the doorway, the first young man—a leader type, Leiv stereotypically pigeon-holed him—turned straight to Glover. Shorter than he or Glover, the young man had a shaved bald head, and a gigantic round earring thing in his left ear.

"Is there going to be a movie theatre coming to town, Chief Deers?" His voice was eager, and sounded to Leiv's ear like the voice of a ten-year-old. *Yep, I'm definitely old as dirt.*

Following the young man was one of the young women, dressed in a long multicolored granny-type skirt, T-shirt with a full chest logo Leiv didn't have a clue who or what it was for, and from what Leiv could see from below her hem and infer from her walking style and sound, he guessed she was clomping around in heavy workman boots. "And my brother wants to know if Amazon or Home Depot are coming to town?" she eagerly asked Glover. Her voice was high, squeaky, and also childish sounding. That's when Leiv noticed the earring in the side of her nose.

Glover smiled a smile of acceptance and accommodation Leiv had never before seen him use—and he was once again awed by Glover's composure, multi-faceted personality, and people-handling abilities. *Always something new.*

For himself, Leiv found the nose-ring very distracting, and hoped the expression on his face did not reveal his distaste. But her eyes were so bright, so intelligent, he was able to focus on those aspects of her countenance, rather than her nose. He doubted, and not for the first time since coming to Shiné, if he could handle being a judge anymore—very unsure if he could remain unbiased in face of current cultural trends.

Following inches behind her, another and taller young man rushed over to Glover. He sported a two-inch tall row of purple spiked hair running down the center of a shaved-to-bald head. *Well, this young man is quite creative,* Leiv thought. Of course he had no idea about those things. Did one select hair colors like you select paint at Home Depot? Try to match or complement your eye color? Immediately Leiv chastised himself—and yet again felt ancient. *And rigid.* He didn't like that part of his self assessment.

"We're caretakers, don't you know," the first young man with the gigantic earring said proudly. "My great-grandfather poured concrete for Main Street. Good friend of LC Rhodes you know."

Who are these people? Leiv realized with an emotional slap in the face, he was doing a darned poor job as steward of LC's legacy town, and was instantly quite ashamed. He didn't remember any of this from LC's journal.

Damn tea, he complained again and wondered if there were any more emotions for him to go through this morning. *No,* he readjusted his assessment, *this isn't the tea. This is my failure to know what's going on around me.*

"And my great-grandfather was a mason on your office, Chief," the taller young man said.

"And my great-grandfather," the third young man behind them chimed in, "Said that there were a lot of squabbles, looking for gold, needing water in some areas, about where roads should be, where the railroad should make stops." Then he pushed himself forward, past the three teenagers already in the room, and added quite proudly, "I saw a man over there who wasn't Lucca."

"Where?" Glover demanded quickly. "And when?"

"Ah, Friday, I think." The bright-eyed teenager, shortest of them all, turned to another new arrival, a gangly-looking young woman, dressed "normally" with no piercings Leiv could see. "You know," the young man asked the young lady for confirmation, "when we were driving down to Dairy Queen?"

She nodded and agreed. "Oh yeah."

"I saw another car, I think, parked on the side of the road heading here just now." The giant-earring young man said.

"A looky-lou probably," the earring-in-her-nose girl said and laughed. "Big deal, a fire. Since there isn't anything else to see out here."

Pastor Apply intruded into their minor-deputy stature-building with The Chief of Police. "One of the suggestions today was for a theatre. With a local drama group. I think you would all like that."

The girl's eyes lit up immediately.

And before Glover could re-claim the conversation, Lloyd also interjected, "Do you know who this gentleman is?"

"I do," the earring girl said smugly, them drew a pantomime zipper across her lips with two fingers.

Two more teenagers had pushed their way into the room. All now stared at Leiv.

"Let me introduce Leigh-Everett Rhodes, grandson of LC Rhodes—the founder of Shiné."

As if in a cartoon, all jaws literally dropped.

"How come we've never met you?" a tentative voice from the back of the "pack" asked.

"Because he doesn't come to church," Lloyd said, then crossed his arms across his chest, and looked pointedly at Leiv.

"Are you a hedonist, then? Cause I heard there's going to be a new nudist colony down the road, too. You could go there."

Leiv laughed out loud, couldn't help it. The thought of him being a "hedonist" in the classical, biblical, or in any sense, was just too darned funny. And a nudist on top of it.

"Hope it won't cost a lot to get in," the purple-haired young man bemoaned.

Nudist camps charge fees?

"Yeah," a tiny voice from the back of the pack said knowingly. "I heard it costs money to get naked."

Leiv waited with Glover outside Shiné Community Church while Adeleine went to the bathroom again.

"I really do think it was the tea." He insisted to Glover. "I've been silly-minded and goofy all morning. And now I know why." He wondered what the Teenage Caretakers meeting inside would think of that.

Glover laughed outright. "Some kind of special Romani Gypsy tea?" he shook his in amusement. "A Russian blend—"

"More like a Hester crazy concoction tea." *Poor David,* Leiv amused himself in thought and words, "David, I'm thinking, is in for some surprises."

"I think you're right." Glover made a head movement in the general direction of his office down main street. "You want some cop-coffee to offset the effect? We can go back to the office and I'll make you some. No funny drugs there."

Leiv knew that Glover's brew, when he made it himself, was strong. Potent. Unfortunately, also full of acid. "I want to go by the hospital and see Lucca." He sighed and felt his face cloud over. "And take a good look at his property."

"Your property actually."

"Yeah, I guess." Leiv didn't want his tiredness to overwhelm him before he had a chance to see Lucca, then afterwards see the damage to Lucca's double-wide. "He's at Barstow hospital? Right? That's at least a couple hour trip."

Glover nodded. "Big responsibility Everett's left you—but we've talked about that before."

"Should have been both of us."

Glover said with a weary sigh, "We've been over that before, Leiv. The property stuff goes all the way back to LC and how he wrote it all." He humphed rather bemusedly, then said,

"Besides, I wouldn't want the mess you're going to have when the County picks one of those projects."

"You think I can stop one of 'them' from doing something here?"

Glover shrugged—then in a seeming change of mind, shook his head. After a moment of silence, he said, "Heck of a guy, our grandfather."

"That he was," Leiv echoed. But he didn't think LC could have anticipated whatever was currently going on. *Whatever it is.*

But Leiv could feel it—just like when he knew a defendant was guilty in his past life. No matter what the jury said.

Now, current day, *something foul was afoot.*

Chapter Six
Pieces in Jeopardy

From LC's journal: I'm thinking these days that I'm kind of special among men for my day. And I'm sometimes wondering what kind of world I'm leaving behind. Sure, I done set it all up, but you never know how the game is going to end up playing out. And which one of my offspring, hoping I'll have plenty, will read my journal and understand? About Viola, about what folks intend, what they really do, and about destinies? Would be nice if I end up in a place where I can look down and see. Specially would like to see how all them trees I planted did. Viola's making sure they get plenty of water while they're babies...

Sunday Still:

"I didn't see nothin'," Lucca said in a weak and mush-mouth sounding voice. Leiv could understand his words though, and was sure Glover, who was even closer, could, too. "One minute...I was walking out to my car...and then I woke up on the ground with Walker pounding on my chest." In a slightly stronger voice, he continued, "Tellin' you Chief, the minute I was back with the living, wanted to punch Walker in the face." He coughed. "Terrible...that would have been. Hitting the man who just saved your life." Lucca lifted his head up an inch or so from his pillow long enough to look straight at Glover standing at the

143

foot of his bed. Leiv was sure the look on Lucca's face conveyed a plea-for-understanding from Glover. "But it hurt like hell, don't you know?"

"It's okay, Mr. Fabero," Glover said quiet soberly. "You didn't hit him. And he's just glad you came back to us."

Leiv was standing back a few feet from Lucca's hospital bed—on the side of the room farthest away from the door. The bed looked to him more like a piece of high-tech robotic equipment than a hospital bed. His spot, out of everyone's way he thought, afforded him a good view of Lucca, and Glover. Leiv figured the reason Glover was now bringing a hand to his face, was to cover a smile he was trying to hide—despite his calm, cool reply to Lucca.

Adeleine did chuckle audibly at Lucca's comment, lowering her chin a bit as she did. She was sitting to Leiv's left, not exactly at the bed, but close enough to see Lucca and take it all in.

Lucca mumbled before collapsing his head back on his pillow, "All happened so fast."

Must have been an accident. Leiv was having a hard time imagining someone would deliberately set Lucca's home on fire. *Such a deliberate act of malice?* Why would someone try to kill his caretaker?

Jasmine was smiling fondly at her dad from her position sitting up close to the other side of his bed—holding his hand. It looked to Leiv like she was barely able to have that little contact, in that Lucca's medical team had him tucked in so he couldn't move—maybe even strapped down if he dared look closer. Visitors could barely see his face. "They" evidently didn't want him to move an inch. It looked like Lucca might actually be squeezing his daughter's hand into his, and not the other way around. His hand being the only body part he could move.

Telltale signs, he thought. Good and bad. The bed and wrappings told Leiv his medical team thought Lucca was not out of the woods. But his managing to talk a bit, and his ability to hang on to his daughter's hand so tightly meant there was determination of spirit in his property caretaker's heart. *And my friend, actually.*

Leiv sighed noiselessly, accompanied by a deep, long, and also noiseless breath. It was a sigh of genuine emotion on his part. Standing there, looking at Lucca, he knew for sure what he felt for the man was genuine. He also knew he had just a few friends in his new Shiné life, and couldn't afford to lose any. And Lucca—well, he hadn't actually realized until the fire, was part of his new little family. Sadly, he hadn't adequately appreciated the man who had become a friend. *Until now. You have to make it, Lucca. You have to.*

As if in answer to Leiv's plea, he heard Lucca's groggy and struggling voice say, "Gasoline near the house."

Leiv turned around abruptly, then took the few steps to the surprisingly expansive hospital room window in back of him. Equally surprising, the view of Barstow from the little hillock the hospital sat on provided a broader-than-expected panorama of this desert gateway town. Los Angeles to the south and west, and Las Vegas to the north and east. The surprising "niceness" of a downhill vista view of Barstow, however, couldn't pull him out of the emotional impact of being in a hospital—or the very real fact of Lucca laying in the bed behind him talking about gasoline.

He contemplated for a few moments what a different world it was from his grandfather's, on so many fronts. Starting with the hospital he was now standing in. New, and from what he could tell, with the latest testing equipment, and monitoring gadgets. Even the latest MRSA control procedures and equipment. LC would be flabbergasted at what medical science could now do.

Nonetheless, and even though Leiv was impressed himself, and for his grandfather—it was still a hospital. With *all* the same unpleasant sensory impacts of *all* the other hospitals he had ever been in.

Even before these moments of consideration standing at Lucca's second floor hospital room window, Leiv wasn't able to stop the memories and emotions whirligigging around in his head that started during their drive in from Shiné.

He could hear in the background, Jasmine's soothing voice behind him, gently prodding Lucca. "Is there anything else you can remember, Dad? Anything at all that could help Chief Deers?"

Glover decided to go see Lucca, too, and he and Adeleine rode into Barstow with him in the back seat of his cruiser. Felt like an eternity, all the way from Shiné to Barstow. *An hour? It* had seemed longer. Leiv now thought back—because of the odd-feeling experience of being in the backseat of a cop car, *and* the additional burden of knowing where they were heading, for sure, emotionally lengthened their journey. It had been a two-headed monster kind of trip. *And also maybe lingering tea effects?*

For the cruiser part—no matter the "ride-along" experiences from his past life—being in the back seat of a cop car always made Leiv feel like he was being carted off to jail. *Funny that,* given his lifelong profession on the other side of the law.

The going-to-the-hospital part was probably worse.

On top of those two spoilers, Adeleine, who was sitting next to him, didn't help matters by proclaiming several times, in several upbeat different ways, "What fun." Evidently, her Illinois experiences never went as far as a cruiser ride, and she found the experience rather exciting. Once again, leaving Leiv feeling "old as dirt"—compared to what he heard as youthful excitement in her voice. *And me now her caretaker of sorts.*

Then there was Glover's driving. Skillful, but fast. Passing whenever he could, even strobing his lights once. Leiv was sure that wasn't kosher—but kept his mouth shut.

Indeed, anxiousness bombarded him from several directions.

Now, looking out over Barstow, having survived the ride in, navigated the seemingly endless hospital corridors, acclimatized as it were to the universal hospital feel, smell, and look—even in Barstow's brand new facility—Leiv still felt a hanging anxiety.

His anxiety was made even worse for knowing Lucca was in the bed behind him—only a couple feet away—still fighting for his life. He had been compelled to visit Lucca. *Duty? Caring? Looking for a puzzle piece? Well,* he concluded, if it were answers he sought at Lucca's bedside, none came.

When they eventually left Lucca's room, Leiv was surprised to find Deputy Tanya Lewis on guard—albeit sitting in a chair across from Lucca's door looking like she was reading a magazine—but "on guard" nonetheless. Leiv was about to say something to her, but saw Glover give the deputy a surreptitious nod of acknowledgement, then quickly turning directly to Leiv, made eye and head movements indicating they should move on down the hall a bit. Not draw attention to Deputy Lewis.

Following Glover's silent instructions, Leiv took Adeleine's arm by way of guiding her, and the three moved away—ten or so feet down the hall from Lucca's room—ending up in-between two patient room doors. There was an elevator door at their end of the hall.

Before letting Glover take control of the situation, Leiv quickly asked, "Deputy Lewis?" He wanted an upfront answer as to "why?" Seemingly, Lucca hadn't revealed anything yet, but Glover and his buddies were guarding his room. To emphasize his desire for a straight answer, Leiv gave Glover a severe and judge-like look. "Is there something more we need to know?"

Adeleine interrupted, "You can fill me in later, Judge. I'm off to find the potty. Can't wait any longer. Very strange," she momentarily put her hand to her stomach, "I think it's that tea...back in a few." And she was gone—down a side-shoot hospital corridor that seemed to just swallow her up.

"Lewis volunteered. Brad Temper is going to relieve her later. Then Walker Johns." He smiled slightly. "I think he's got a crush on Jasmine," he said, with his John Wayne cowboy evocative tone. "But he respects that she's married." He shook his head, again John Wayne style, and added. "Poor kid."

Leiv refrained from mentioning Walker was not in the "kid" stage of life.

Glover next noisily blew out his breath and made an exasperated face. "Just don't like houses burning up like that right under my nose. And Shiné residents ending up in the hospital. Don't think that fire was an accident. Not something Lucca would accidently let happen."

"Surely you've had fires out here before? Before I came back—"

"Oh yeah, but they just don't burn like that. Even some of the dirt was charred? Like something was poured directly on it. Starting in the front of the house—not in back of the kitchen or the shed-kinda shop-structure Lucca had out back."

"So you think it was arson?"

"Yes, I think it's possible someone was trying to kill him. Didn't you hear Lucca? Means he must have smelled gasoline right before he passed out."

He waited as Glover took a long moment before adding, "I don't know what I think for sure, but I'm not taking any chances. Waiting for the Fire Chief's report."

Leiv looked around, hoping for another window like Lucca's to the outside world. He saw one at the end of corridor, but it was in the direction away from the elevator.

Glover said, "And Jasmine's husband Tim is coming later this afternoon to relieve her at Lucca's side."

Despite the unpleasant circumstances—and *wanting* to escape the hospital environment, and *wanting* Lucca to be okay and back sitting in his double-wide happily doing what caretakers do, and *wanting* to protect Adeleine—Leiv nonetheless, felt the corners of his mouth forming a wee smile as his mind's eye envisioned a naked nudist colony man sitting by Lucca's bed.

On the way back to Shiné, both Glover and Adeleine seemed subdued—and Leiv thought he understood why. They were all three assessing the circumstances they just left. For at least an hour or so, they endured not being able to escape from the permeating smell and feel of "hospital," and the reality of seeing and talking to Lucca—wrapped up as he was like a mummy in that high-tech bed-thing, barely able to talk. A sobering experience, indeed.

Leiv turned his attention outside, trying to take in all the "little things" along I-40 he missed when he drove the stretch himself. *Forget the hospital.* And from his individual perspective, Leiv also hoped the effects of Hester's "Tin Can Madness" had worn off by now.

Holding his gaze to the passing terrain, he did manage a smile at his name for the contents of the can in Rhodes-Castle's kitchen. "Tin Can Madness" had popped into his brain on the fly as they started to head eastward on I-40 out of Barstow—*back to my Shiné refuge.* His emotions now sought calmness and clarity from the fall world outside of his cruiser confinement. It was a time for him to digest all the bits-and-pieces that had come his way since yesterday—*so much in so few hours*—trying to fit them together to somehow make sense.

Still, and no matter how hard he tried, Twenty-Nine Palms Logistics Base hospital forced itself forward into his conscious thoughts. *Evidently hospital memories last forever.* And there it was, front and center, the very similar and distasteful institutional feelings he just experienced at Barstow Hospital.

But now, in the back seat of Glover's cruiser, Leiv realized for the first time in his life the possibility there might be people who didn't like being in government buildings—courthouses and courtrooms in particular. *Yet, I loved them.* Those buildings and those rooms had been his home-away-from-home.

Indeed, the hospital bundle of emotions was probably home for many.

He also knowingly allowed himself the smug and self-righteous pleasure of would-be know-it-alls—having an idea, examining it, and still retaining his biased position in the light of supposed rational examination. Now in the back seat of Glover's cruiser, Leiv thought, *such arrogance on my part.* He held to his bias anyway—from his past, and now; hospitals sucked, and courthouses didn't.

When they were finally nearing the Shiné turnoff, and while still silently peering out his side window, Leiv realized he was squinting even more intensely. For around the Newberry Springs exit, they'd driven into a maelstrom of sand consisting of swirling dust devils larger than any he had yet seen—charging down the median strip as if being chased—eastward bound. He should have paid attention on the way into Barstow when sight conditions were better—but now, he wanted to see the culvert where Glover's cop friend found a dead body.

Leiv needn't have worried, as there were still several barricades and a CHP vehicle onsite. The culvert would have been hard to miss. He noticed Glover slowed down a bit, even though traffic was light. *Maybe with similar thoughts.* Of course, he'd been there already. Leiv turned his gaze from outside his backseat window to look at Glover.

Glover's wide-brimmed hat was on the front seat next to him, yet all Leiv could see was the back of his head—and with that, another one of his "never to be forgotten" memories flooded over him.

They were on their way to Twenty-Nine Palms, and on the side of the road in the aftermath of their having been shot at incident last winter. Leiv had pulled Glover's head to his chest, and was reassuring him, "The Marine's are coming, Dusty, the Marines are coming." He thought he might be rocking, but wasn't sure. "Hang in there, hang in there. The Marine's are coming." *Just last winter. The Marine base hospital.*

Leiv shook his head, banishing the event from their shared past and returned his attention to the dust bowl freeway Glover was now hopefully leaving as he turned north, heading back home to Shiné.

My refuge? Hardly right now. Leiv knew for sure there was more coming. And soon.

"Now that I'm here in Shiné," Adeleine said, "I'm not sure what I'm supposed to do."

Glover looked at Leiv, his expression asking, *"Well, what the heck should she be doing?"*

"I don't know," Leiv answered honestly. It was for sure, a question he needed to answer soon. "All I know is, I need to keep you safe."

She made a face he didn't know how to interpret. Then Adeleine shook her head, "It all happened so fast. Father all but forcing me." She blew out an exasperated breath. "You saw, all I brought was one small suitcase." She looked down, then brushed her thighs. "I'll have to wash these jeans soon. Is there a clothing store in town?"

Leiv and Glover said almost in unison, "No." Glover added alone, "My mother buys almost everything through the internet. We have very good delivery service."

"Post Office?"

"Not here, but in Newberry Springs and Baker. And UPS and FedEx come here without any problem. Easy off I-Forty and I-Fifteen."

"If you're into vintage dresses," Leiv added, "Mary Jones at *Le Bric-à-Brac* often has some items." Surprisingly, he thought she looked excited at the prospect of bygone era dresses.

Leiv had left his truck parked in front of Shiné's Chief of Police office while they went to Barstow Hospital. Now returned, the three of them were sitting at Glover's desk drinking his freshly made brew. An emotional time-out.

Glover's brew tasted excellent, but for Leiv, it was actually the coffee aroma defining the moment. Someway, somehow, the unique bouquet of aromas Glover's special blend coffee exuded, was not only calming—but physically and mentally sobering. He needed that.

"I shouldn't have let him drag me out here," she murmured with what sounded to Leiv like half-hearted bravado.

Glover asked her what Leiv was thinking. "What else could you have done?"

"I should have gotten out at one of our pit-stops."

"Rest areas?"

She nodded.

"And what would you have done then?" Glover pushed her. "Hitched?"

"Well, well...."

Glover sighed, leaned back more comfortably in his desk swivel chair, and eyed them both.

Bemused, Leiv thought, *he's looking at us like delinquent teenagers he's dragged in because our parents asked him.*

"Ms. Moore," Glover said, "I barely know you. But listening to everything you and Leiv have said, for my part, having more experience than I'd ever want with amoral scumbags and determined politicians...." He paused several seconds to afford leaning forward and staring even harder at them, "And guessing as to fatherly-intentions, I'd say your father has tried—in his own unique way—to get you out of harm's way."

Then Glover nailed him in particular, with a stare Leiv had seen before and hadn't particularly cared for. "And you, my friend, have been charged with protecting Ms. Moore. Like it or not."

Annoyingly, Leiv felt his face warm—hadn't happened very often in his past life. "I know. But how the heck can we…I…do that? It's possible Adeleine's clear out of danger now, and it's also possible there's another hired gunman—"

Glover interrupted, "'Fixer' he's called."

Leiv waved his hand dismissively. "Whatever he's called." Then in a gesture to stop Glover from interrupting again, "We just can't take any chances. This "fixer" person could be headed to California right now to kill Adeleine and anyone associated with her."

He looked to Adeleine and saw fear in her eyes. In a calmer voice, Leiv added, "Unlikely, but we can't ignore the possibility until we get word there's no one else out there."

After a couple of seconds of silence, he next said, and now looking at Glover, "Just like you're doing with the guard outside Lucca's door. Not until we know how burning down Lucca's home fits into all this, we can't take any chances."

"You're right." Glover nodded his head.

Adeleine also nodded in agreement, and swiped at several escaping tears. Leiv hoped his tone of voice hadn't prompted them—but guessed they had. He figured it was also the predicament she was finding herself in adding a few tears of frustration. *Winston's callous doing. No matter how much Glover tries to gloss over it.*

Leiv turned his head away from them both and looked out Glover's storefront window. Out onto his grandfather's Main Street. And in line with the flip-flopping his mind had obstinately done all morning, Leiv wondered if Le Bric-à-Brac was even open—and if Mary Jones had any preferences regarding how Shiné should change.

Is that Doc Walker getting out of his car and going into Mary's antique shop? It was the doc indeed, and Leiv wondered at the possibility of even more romance in the air. *As if Hester Miller and David Milhouse aren't providing enough excitement in the "love" arena.*

* * * * *

"I wonder who that was pulling off the gravel shoulder?" Adeleine asked from the passenger seat of Leiv's truck.

Dusk had fallen and it was hard to see. "Probably somebody who had just stopped to check something. Like their map. Or cell phone."

Leiv was only half paying attention to the car—his mind and heart being captured by the darkening scene to his left at Lucca's. It was a different world from just two days ago, and it was taking him some moments to take in the devastation again. Didn't like this happening in *his* town.

Yes, more and more he was recognizing "this place" as home. Especially after all the other new items today's events heaped on him—*as if yesterday weren't enough.* His perspective was shifting—acknowledging he had Shiné caretaker responsibilities passed down from his grandfather. His inner self was moving and changing—without asking his consent.

"A lot of Roadies come this way." Leiv squinted and forced his eyes from the taped-off and sign-marked scene to his left so he could catch a decent glimpse of the car going down the road ahead of them. "And he's headed toward I-40." What he saw was the tail end of a white sedan type car. Leiv knew he wasn't good at identifying auto models, and the car was moving away too fast for him to get a plate number.

Although, in the last instance of his glance, Leiv thought he additionally saw a red pickup truck pull out of the bushes halfway between them and the disappearing white sedan. Also going south toward I-40. But Leiv wasn't sure if his eyes were playing tricks on him—what with the blowing winds, sands, sagebrush, and falling darkness. Leiv returned his attention to the land across the road—Lucca's former home.

Adeleine said, "It's awful isn't it? You know, this was all happening when we arrived Saturday." She made a self-deprecating sound. "Of course you know that, too. I remember us watching you come up your drive toward us. Father and me and Malcolm waiting for you. You couldn't help but see it."

"Yeah." Leiv pulled off onto a piece of shoulder where he thought his truck wouldn't be in the way—a stop just before the official fire line started. This strip of drivable dirt which offered access to the property, ran for about one-hundred feet or so along the two-lane highway. Now, completely closed off with bright-yellow streaming fire line tape, printed with "Keep Out" in big black letters—and running between three sawhorse-styled sign hangers. There were also highway-style signs in front of each sawhorse that read—"Keep Out," "Firemen at Work," and "No Access."

"Can't miss this...Saturday, on our way to town, or to Barstow today...or right now," he murmured. "Just awful."

Once Leiv turned off his truck's motor, they both made the necessary movements to get out and go behind the fire line.

Suddenly it was dead calm. No wind. No birds chirping. Nothing.

"This is your property, right?" she asked, as they walked and stumbled—even sliding a little in the still soggy fire-zone aftermath.

"Well, my grandfather's." Leiv immediately recognized how stupid that sounded. "Of course he's dead."

"And your father, Everett too. You know I met him in Chicago when we went up there once."

That surprised Leiv. "You must have been a baby. How could you remember?" He forced back his Shiné memory of being at his father's side. His death bed. Holding his hand. Promising his father he'd move back to Shiné himself. Leiv had thought at the time his promise was a death bed kindness—and a lie. *Yet, here I am.*

Adeleine had put on a hoodie she'd dragged with her out of the truck, zipped it up, and tied down the hood part—leaving only the main features of her face visible. When Leiv turned to help her, he almost laughed.

Seeing something in his face or hearing something in his voice, she said, "You know I'm not as young as you think I am. Or want me to be."

He wasn't sure how to take the last bit, but figured she was backhandedly calling him old. Remembering the teenagers at Shiné community church, he chided himself that everyone lately was looking like a child to him, and suspected the opposite was also true.

"You know, Judge, I'm really surprised by all the trees." She looked around where they were as if she could orientate herself. "And Lucca said something about figs and pears, I think."

"LC planted them...the trees around the property." He stopped, catching himself before his voice caught as he remembered the passage in LC's journal where he talked about Viola helping him plant and water trees on what he called his "near in" property. Leiv thought himself good at catching and not displaying emotional surprises—had to be as a judge. But today was really throwing him for a loop. *Hester's damnable tea.*

"The figs and pears were Lucca touches." All the Athols and pines along the road looked surprisingly well. *Tough like LC.* "We'll have to look around some more if the crew still here will let us. Lucca's prized trees might have survived." He doubted his supposition. "Who would do such a thing?"

"You don't think it was an accident?"

Leiv let her question hang a few seconds before answering, "No—no accident. Lucca's too savvy to just let something like this happen."

Part Two

Facit Justitia
Let justice be done

Chapter Seven
Endgames in Retrospect

From LC's journal: *Sometimes, I got to take the time to sit and think. Figure out if what I've been doing is going to work. Figure out what I regret, and how to do it different next time. Viola says I don't ponder enough. I'm a changing that. She says "Learn from your mistakes, LC."*

Looking back on Sunday Night:

Leiv was alone in his copula safe haven Monday morning. "I'm happy for you, HM," he told his private and silent special world atop Rhodes Castle. Of course he couldn't actually reveal his feeling to the woman herself. "And I forgive you for the psychedelic tea." He smiled at his added quip.

He knew Hester Miller hadn't much liked him—*maybe still doesn't*—but he had yet to sort out his feelings for her. Indeed, just last winter she tried to steal his grandfather's Mojave-Stone. His ambiguity of emotions notwithstanding, her finding a true love and happiness with the most unexpected partner he could have imagined, was a marvelous happening in the way of the world known to him. Schmaltzy thinking he figured, but who was to know he allowed himself such a sappy moment? *Up here in LC's private viewing room to the world.*

For him, this cupola was a special place in Rhodes Castle.

He was very fond of its large-paned plain glass windows—like the one he was standing in front of—watching yet another brilliant red and tangerine horizon develop before him. *And the brushed-like wisps of light blue floating through its otherwise high-hued beauty.* He chuckled to himself at his flowery sunrise descriptions. Victorian thoughts and HM tolerance—all because the sun rose yet another day in the Mojave. *Residual Hester-tea effects?*

His amusement turned to a pleasant sigh as he changed his viewpoint to the more south-facing copula window. Indeed, the top-of-the-castle room was quite different from most of the castle—clear uninterrupted views. Completely different from the stained glass surrounding the entryway double doors, and the even more intricately-cut and brilliantly-colored windows guarding both sides of the massive fireplace in LC's "withdrawing" room.

He was glad he'd come up to the top to witness the day begin. As the sky colors continued to develop, he sat down on the window seat of this particular window and accompanying view—one of five—all with their unique perspectives of Shiné and the Mojave.

After checking Adeleine was still sleeping, Leiv had initially started his morning quite early, still in PJ's and robe, in pre-dawn darkness in his library staring out the library's massive window to the world—gazing at the stars and gigantic fall moon against what seemed like a flat photographic projection on a flat black background. *Sometimes the sky seems curved.* Fleetingly, he wondered what made the difference. Atmosphere or him?

His view, however, from his second floor library was not all-encompassing as with the copula where he finally ended up. *But still dramatic*—especially for enjoying the solid blackness of Shiné nights. He had sat in his father's armed-desk-chair at LC's desk, preparing to stay until morning was full on.

But for some reason, in the library, contrary to his initial expectation, and even with a full-moon sky, Leiv couldn't seem to touch his father through the furnishings like he often did. Even surrounded with past-century ambiance and multi-generational emotional touchstones—the link just wasn't there.

He couldn't even seem to connect with himself. His floor to ceiling glass-fronted bookcases were indeed jammed full with his legal tomes. He'd shipped much of his Illinois law library to Shiné—some he'd given away, but not a lot. Most, he would probably never read again, some, not even open again. Comfort-possessions, he'd realized on several occasions. Books, when needed, he could feel, touch, smell—and be reminded of the man who'd sat on the bench in Illinois for so many years.

Before leaving his library for the castle's copula, one thing Leiv did internalize—the room was now *his* library, and he said aloud to the library, "Thank you father. Thank you grandfather."

Indeed, his schmaltzy thoughts about Hester had started in the library as he watched the horizon infinitesimally brighten—from jet black to midnight-blue. Leiv envisioned the picture of HM and David—*such an incomprehensible matchup,* sitting on a Hollywood set as was David's job—gauging the appropriateness of the set's furnishings and accoutrements. But— when he tried thinking of HM and David actually being lovey-dovey, holding hands and kissing—Leiv still couldn't bring up an image.

The sound of a phone ringing downstairs somewhere in the house brought Leiv back to the present here and now in LC's copula. And unfortunately, he couldn't ignore the ringing phone even from his safe haven. *Who the hell was calling? And why?*

Finally, Leiv remembered Adeleine. He had a "guest" he needed to take care of—and the sound from the phone suddenly went from annoying to menacing. *Especially after last night.* Then he remembered her mentioning Winston was supposed to call this morning. Indeed, Leiv waited, and after several rings the phone stopped. She had picked up and answered what was probably her father's call.

He could continue re-living the rest of his Sunday.

Just yesterday afternoon....

After their walk around and experiencing the fire aftermath at Lucca's —and feeling a bit overwhelmed by the devastation, Leiv drove back across the road, and up LC's long steep driveway. He parked in his usual spot in front of the carriage house, where both he and Adeleine declared almost simultaneously—they both needed naps. Even though evening was upon them.

However, once inside, Leiv didn't feel comfortable completely abandoning his "watching over" Adeleine duties by heading straight to his bedroom and collapsing. Consequently, after she went up to *her* new bedroom—LC's comfortable suite— Leiv opted to stretch out on the couch in the TV room. *The Parlor*, as LC had named the room right off the front entry. During Hester's reign, she had watched TV in her quarters, while he would watch in this room.

Leiv had also occasionally accepted business-type guest visits in the parlor, instead of the massive withdrawing room, or even the more relaxed kitchen. He thought of the TV room more like a "living room" in his generational vernacular. Glover called it a "family room," stating emphatically, and on more than one occasion, "If you bring in a TV, you've entered another room-naming realm."

Not for Leiv. Admittedly he had added the modern large-screen TV and a plush modern easy chair designed for TV watching and lounging—but the antique cream-colored Riccoco parlor settee set, and the dark Victorian-blue walls above rich walnut stained Victorian designed wainscoting affixed the sitting room in Leiv's mind as "LC's Victorian Parlor dream." TV or not. *Or was it Viola's dreams that ran throughout Rhodes-Castle?* Leiv had read LC's entire diary many times now. Still, he wasn't sure.

Regardless whether the parlor-cum-TV-room was his grandfather or grandmother's vision, Leiv figured that here, after such a day, he would only fall half-asleep. So stretching out as best he could given the couch's length—Leiv allowed his eyes to close just a tad. He was sound asleep within seconds.

* * * * *

When he woke up, mentally disorganized and slightly startled—the house seemed unnaturally noiseless. Of course, the castle was often quiet these days, what with Hester and Dobie elsewhere. But somehow this was different. *Adeleine?* He needed to find her. *Maybe she's still napping.* However rational this thought was, Leiv's brain translated the silence into "danger."

Instantly he was up, left the parlor, and started calling her name out loudly—first in the direction of the front entry, then down the hall toward the back along the staircase.

Finally he heard low-level noises in the kitchen he couldn't immediately identify. Familiar, but not entirely. Quickly, Leiv rushed down the hall to the back of the house, and Hester's kitchen. *No,* not Hester's anymore. *I need to adjust my thinking.* Regardless of kitchen-ownership in his mind, Leiv's body still hurried until he was finally able to push open the kitchen door and actually see Adeleine moving around—wiping off countertops, rearranging.

Hearing him enter, she looked up and smiled. "I couldn't sleep any longer. But I really didn't know what to do."

Leiv's alarm bells had subsided.

Now remembering in the privacy of Rhodes Castle's copula, Leiv could once again see Adeleine sitting at the kitchen table clear as if it were happening again...hear her voice.

"What a Sunday we've had," he had mused aloud.

"You can say that again," she agreed, her tone thoughtful.

Starting with being walked-out-on by Glover at TGS, *then* the fire at Lucca's, *then* Winston's out of the blue appearance, *then* the community kerfuffle he'd painfully sat through, *then* the drive to Barstow and their sobering visit at the hospital—*then* finally inspecting Lucca's destroyed home and scorched land "up close and personal."

Sure, it was actually his land, handed down through his grandfather, but Leiv's mind and emotions identified that little piece of Shiné with Lucca.

Lucca's land.

Adeleine had smiled—a mix of whimsy and curious concern. "Not what I was expecting to experience out here in the desert. But exciting for sure." He thought she looked more rested than he felt, and seemingly rather accepting of her new Shiné adventure.

"Not stuff I was expecting either. And I live here." Indeed, this latest *strangeness* all started for him at TGS—and his finally wanting to explain to Glover about the Mojave-Stones. "Whatever is going on," he shared his thought aloud, "It all started Saturday for me."

They'd just finished cups of coffee she'd made in the French-press Hester never used. *Strong and good*, Leiv thought. As for Hester's tea brew, and his consequential mental experiences— Leiv wasn't sure if he would *ever* drink tea again. Of any kind. He knew of course he would, but his morning out-of-control mental shenanigans had put him off "having a cuppa'" for awhile.

Sunday night, the coffee had been perfect for the time and place—and he now thought Adeleine possessed good instincts in that hot caffeinated evening drink.

Full-on darkness had fallen for sure during his nap as days were shorter now; still, *Sunday ended so soon*, it seemed. A good and bad occurrence.

Leiv had impulsively asked, "Do you want to see what Shiné night skies are like?" He wanted Adeleine to see what he saw in Mojave night skies, feel what he felt—experience "his" desert sky with him.

"You have to train your eyes, but if you just look out toward the trees, you can actually see those Athols. Blackest of the black shadows moving in the wind." He and Adeleine were protected from nighttime gusts sitting on Everett and LC's bench—the trees absorbing the brunt of the winds. He fell silent and waited. Taking in the night.

After a long moment, Adeleine said softly, "Yes, I can see them." Then after another stretch of companionable silence, "And quiet. Like in the cornfields."

Leiv's remembered Illinois cornfields never seemed this dark, but quiet, yes. He accepted her analogy and added, "Inside the castle, and outside here." He had spoken almost in a whisper. "There's a strange noiselessness sometimes." Sounded silly, he knew.

But Adeleine said, "I know what you mean. Kind of ominous, even." She shivered slightly underneath her hoodie. The hood part was again pulled up and tightly snuggled her face. Her arms were wrapped around her body.

"Glad you bundled up?" Leiv had suggested bringing her hoodie along. For himself, he'd grabbed his heavy Eddie Bauer down jacket—and patted his pocket when putting it on to make sure he had LC's gun with him.

She nodded. "Thanks for mentioning. Didn't realize it would be so cold."

"I have another heavier one like mine if you need it."

"Thanks, I'm okay for now."

"You know, like you mentioned earlier, I first saw you, Everett, and Malcolm sitting right here. Waiting for me."

No matter the temperature, Leiv was comfortable when sitting on LC and Everett's bench—*now mine.* "You want to hear the story about this bench?"

He could feel her nod again. Then after another moment of amiable silence but before he had his thoughts together enough to tell his bench story, Adeleine said, "This *is* a nice spot. With the trees sort of hiding the bench, and the way you can look straight up into the sky if you want, and without anyone knowing you're doing it." She rubbed her hand along the front of her bench section. "And the feel of the bench's wood when you run your hand along it." She sighed pleasurably. "Did you add this bench?

His turn to nod.

"So, what *is* the story?"

"The trees—Athols they're called—do provide a good hedge to the west side of the front door and the driveway. Some are twenty to thirty feet away from the house itself even though it doesn't seem like it. And the wall makes it amazingly private. Except from the view I had yesterday morning of you guys." He had taken a moment to remember and smiled mischievously to himself in the darkness. "The feeling when sitting here isn't exactly like a bench in a maze, but when I was a kid, I easily imagined one."

Leiv proceeded to tell her the bench's history. How LC had built his castle with the huge trees in mind, making sure they weren't damaged. Then planted even more. And about the day when his father Everett—while LC was still alive—had the teak English garden bench delivered "from somewhere to their west." He told Adeleine how Everett had supervised the workmen in the particulars of an exact placement of the special bench—as to maintain privacy among the trees, but close enough to the house to afford a view of night skies above the trees.

In the retelling to Adeleine, Leiv was once again reminded of his emotional attachment to "this little bench," and how glad he was LC had still been alive to appreciate Everett's efforts. *Yes,* Leiv knew LC was quite pleased. *Enough to write it down in his diary.*

And at the time of the bench's inaugural sitting, Leiv could still hear his father's spoken words, *"You sit on it first, Leigh-Everett," he had said.* It was the first night after the bench was in place. Then his father held his hand while they watched the night stars together. Leiv had felt a lump in his throat rise Sunday night, and now again, remembering this Monday morning.

It was black-dark by then, and Leiv had hoped Adeleine hadn't seen the emotion that must have appeared on his face. In that Sunday night darkness, he next looked up toward what he expected to be another star-studded clear Mojave desert night. Instead, he saw a muted, unusually starless and matte-blue blackness hanging over them in the far distance.

"But it's not cloudy?" he whispered. This was a new experience for him, and he wasn't quite sure how to explain what the heavens were doing to confuse him. And why?

"What's the matter?" Adeleine asked.

"Funny looking sky."

She followed his gaze and looked up again.

Then out of nowhere—an unpleasantness creeped into his being, manifesting itself first in the back of his neck, followed by an accompanying chill running down his back. He pulled his jacket in closer and crossed his arms to warm himself. *Or to ward off something?*

The line of Athols and their eerie shadows stopped moving. And in that quiet, Leiv thought he heard a car go down the road. *Unusual this time of night.* The motor sound was slight, as if the driver was going slow.

His arms still wrapped across his midriff, Leiv rubbed both of his upper arms.

Then silence again.

He waited.

Maybe another motor? Gunning it? What the hell was going on?

Leiv almost got up to walk down his drive and see what he could see—but then he felt in his pocket. His grandfather's M1911 was there, though the metal, like him, was cold—but comforting indeed. His duty was to stay here and protect Adeleine. Curiosity would have to take a backseat this time. He needed to be Adeleine's caretaker—*right here, right now.*

In retrospect, in the morning's clarifying brightness and warming comfort of Rhodes Castle copula, Leiv shook himself back into the present. Last night and its possible intrigue were past. *No,* he had needed to hang around and protect Adeleine. Duty first—*curiosity second.* Monday morning—and the world was beginning again. This morning he was sure LC's cave voice wanted him to be there at Adeleine's side last night no matter what lurked outside LC and Everett's special Athol hideaway.

And, that was yesterday.

Then he addressed himself aloud in the solitude atop Rhodes Castle with the admonishment, "Leigh-Everett Rhodes now needs to deal with today, and today's dangers." *And pleasures.* Hester's wedding was only a blink away.

Looking back on Sunday Night:

Monday morning—a workday for most, and consequently Caltrans workers were back at the job on the I-40 median strip. CHP Officer Ben Belleau was also back on construction-site babysitting duty. This morning, however, he didn't mind— actually glad for the time to think and go back over yesterday's events. *Especially after last night.*

After spotting the squirrelly looking guy from the pass and at Penny's Sunday morning, Ben didn't have time to immediately confirm his hunches with more detective work. A five-car pileup on I-15 in the southwest bound lanes pulled him back to one of his designated CHP duties. He and a Mojave County Sheriff's Deputy in Yermo were the closest, and consequently were first on scene.

There were no serious injuries, but now there were five car owners, and several other driver-witnesses to take statements from. After *in situ* details were recorded, *and after* a tow-truck and human-labor assistance finally got everyone onto the shoulder, *and after* all official accident reports were completed—Ben then ended up directing traffic around the accident.

He had volunteered, wanting to scan the cars and faces. He just couldn't get the guy from the pass out of his mind. The accident was on a four-lane stretch on I-15, leaving only one southwest bound lane open for flow-through traffic until everything was cleared up. The Deputy, and now another CHP officer Ben had met—but didn't really know—collected scene-info, witness statements, and future contact details while he directed traffic. The stop-and-go backup went for miles, but most drivers were okay with the situation. *Las Vegas winners?*

Ben figured it would be extraordinary to see that same rental car driver again. But stranger things had happened in his career. *Sometimes a look, a glance, an unexpected sighting—a "tell."*

Hours passed however before the freeway was back to normal—with no lucky sighting. So, by the time his shift was over—and admittedly on a hunch—and after going back to the station to get his pickup, Ben then drove all the way back to the Mojave. Once in the Yermo-Daggett area, beginning at Penny's, he started cruising the area for the car and the man while it was still light enough to see. His search was fruitless.

Finally, knowing dusk would be falling soon, and while driving south through Shiné—planning to loop his way back home on I-40—Ben stopped at Chief of Police Glover Deers's office. Figured he should at least thank him for taking on the body in the culvert. Glover might even have some subsequent information to share.

After parking and getting out of his cruiser in front of Glover's office, Ben did take a moment to look around, see if he could feel anything good about this podunk place—and oddly, in the glow of a startling red pre-sunset sky starting to spread across Lookout Loop outcropping, it wasn't half bad. He could almost see why Glover Deers plunked himself down in this spot. The wind had momentarily stopped, and the air even smelled decent.

But all that was yesterday. Now, this Monday morning, once again back on median-construction-site duty, his remembered experiences seemed rather fantastical. Ben shook his head at the environmental contrast—then and now—then let his thoughts go back and continue to reexamine his Sunday night happenings.

The Chief had met him at the front door of his storefront office.

"Just thought I'd stop by on my way home," Ben said. He didn't expect Glover knew where home was for him, or his work schedule, so it didn't matter which direction he'd parked his red pickup right out front. No cause for Glover to wonder about his arrival in approaching darkness.

"Glad you did," Glover said. "But a little surprised. Didn't think you liked our part of the Mojave that much."

"Don't know what gave you that idea," he answered sardonically while following Glover inside, then over to his desk.

Glover gestured toward the chair by his desk, "I'm heading out soon myself, but can I offer you some coffee? It's not that stale and I can microwave—"

"No, no." Ben held up his hand. He'd had quite enough coffee for the day—starting with that morning at Penny's restaurant, then out of the Deputy Sheriff's thermos at the accident site. "Just wanted to stop by and make sure you knew everything we know about that body in the culvert I dumped on you." He then proceeded to give Glover the minimum he could. He liked Glover, and though he dumped *his* dead body on him, he knew how bulldoggish Glover could be, and didn't want him fretting over something he couldn't do anything about.

Glover surprised him with, "Well, I can add a little to your profile." Then he proceeded to fill Ben in with the information he had.

Ben had been quite amazed. "You may be out here in the farthest reaches of no man's land, but you've evidently got good sources." He was hoping Glover would share who and how he found out about the hit men.

He'd watched as Glover's expression turned enigmatic. No such luck on source revelation. The Chief of Police did, however, provide him with some information he didn't have—and from quite an unexpected direction. Information which helped him understand why the man he suspected was The Fixer, was at Penny's this morning eating breakfast. And further justified his own plans.

Evidently, a Leiv Rhodes was protecting the possible victim. "Says something good about this local man on several fronts. That this Illinois bigwig trusts him in the first place, and that he's willing to take on the role."

"Yeah, he's okay. Used to be a Judge, you know." Glover had straightened his back, and leaned conspiratorially across his desk—in closer toward him. "Telling you all of this so you'll keep an eye out when you're in the area." Glover must have picked up something from the expression on his face, because he added, "Highly unlikely you'd be cruising Main Street if you don't have to." Glover chuckled affably, "Except like if you have to pass through to get home. But just in case."

"You're right about that," Ben agreed while realizing Glover was sharper than he expected. Ben also got the feeling Glover and Rhodes must be friends. But he didn't explore the issue. Instead, he looked outside, saw night was fully upon them, and decided to get moving.

Now it was Monday morning, and he was sitting on the I-40 median, the wind kicking up again, dust starting to fly and roll—*damn desert*. Ben sighed heavily and said to the interior of his Dodge Charger cruiser, "That was just the beginning of last night."

Now, Ben Bellaeu knew he needed to deal with today, and today's tasks—starting with the emotional acceptance of what Ben considered monumental regrets from the rest of Sunday night.

* * * * *

Looking back on Sunday Night:

Glover liked living on the back of his mother's property. He was close enough to keep an eye out for her while having his own privacy; and she retained the feeling of being alone and independent. Of course she would be appalled to know he was "keeping an eye out."

Glover set his own schedule—so often they would have early morning coffee together at her house—her cats, Samara and Silky in faithful attendance. But not this Monday morning. If there was a police emergency, Shiné residents knew to call 911 and they would find him. For now, Glover just wanted to lean back in his rocker on his A-frame's front porch, orientate himself eastward toward the rising sun and developing horizon colors; while counterproductively to actually appreciating said horizon—close his eyes, and think for a bit more.

Especially after Sunday night.

Starting with reliving Officer Ben Bellaeu's visit. Glover remembered he didn't immediately rush off after Ben left, though he had wanted to get home before his mother and her cats were engrossed in their TV watching. He liked saying "Hi" before heading off to "his place."

He had also needed to complete his ritual office shutdown before closing up. While he went around making sure all doors were locked, checking the coffeepot was off, and the paper files and gun safes were locked—Glover had let his mind consider several nagging items.

Starting off with the fact he'd done background homework and information requests not only for the murdered man—but also for CHP Officer Ben Bellaeu. Exactly why he had, Glover wasn't yet sure.

Just a hunch, he had thought then, and again this morning. Consequently, Glover knew Bellaeu lived in Rosamond, in Kern County, and stopping by his Shiné office on his way home was a fabrication. So why was he really in the area? And why stop in to see him even if he was? Pick his brain for information, was his first guess. But could it be for some reason he needed to figure out? A reason that affected him or Shiné?

Rather inexplicably so far, somewhere in the "put two-and-two together" part of his brain, Glover had slotted Ben in as a possible for the "vigilante" that multi-state task forces were scouring several counties searching for. He didn't really want to think Ben was their guy, it was an "out there" theory, and one that gave him a perverse dichotomy of emotions. Speculating cops were looking for a cop. *Justice and law-enforcement,* juxtaposing and competing concepts he had thought about in the past. Even discussed with Leiv several times over snifters of Harvey's Bristol Crème. *Wish Leiv would stock whiskey instead.*

Though what Officer Ben Bellaeu's role in all of this was, he might need to let slide for awhile. *Wait and watch.* Having proof, not just a hunch was what he needed. It was the legal structure he'd bought into, *what I believe in and stand for.* Proof.

Then there was the fire site at Lucca's. It *felt* like arson to him. But, once again, just a hunch. Neither San Bernardino nor Needles CSI had presented any information suggesting arson. So far, probably accidental. *A gasoline can with escaping fumes, maybe?* On top of that, who would want to kill Lucca? What did he have someone wanted? Or hate him for?

During his final office walk-around last night, Glover's ponderings moved on to all those goofy proposals to the county for Shiné enhancements. *Funny,* in that he really didn't want Shiné to change. *To grow?* At the same time, did he actually want Shiné to stay the way it was? *A "Rhodes" town?* Both were possibilities, and he had yet to figure out where he stood. Finally, he turned off the lights and locked the front door, then pulled and locked the grates across the glass windows and door.

Glover's parting consideration when getting into his cruiser to head home—intending to leave all things police related for Monday morning revisiting—was that he liked Ben. *Good cop in so many respects.* Notwithstanding dumping a dead body on him. Glover smiled, remembering running off from TGS Sunday morning leaving a very irritated Leiv behind.

Now this Monday morning, Glover could feel in his cop bones, especially after everything yesterday and then last night, that today was special. He almost opened his eyes ready to take on the day. But his rocker was so comfortable.

A special day if not for him, but maybe for the players playing *their* games around him? His mother Margaret's often shared words of wisdom. *"Watch out for other people's games...."* Indeed, he overheard her counsel Leiv with the same philosophy after the community hullabaloo yesterday. Thinking back now, he also wasn't sure what to think about the community meeting. *Maybe a community garden, desert or otherwise ....*

Instead, he squeezed his eyes closed even tighter, as if the activity itself would help him re-visualize the scene he really wanted to ponder—*re-see* the two cars he thought he saw pulling away from Lucca's land last night. He was pretty darned sure that was what he saw on his way home. *Well, not positive.* It was indeed dark. He had almost switched on his strobe and siren. *But for what reason?* It certainly wasn't an infraction to stop on the side of the road. Especially to use a cell phone or coordinating between two cars traveling together.

Finally, Glover opened his eyes. *But that was last night.* The sunrise he now saw was pretty nice by his way of thinking. He pulled himself up straight in his rocker and planted his feet firmly on the deck. "Chief Glover Deers needs to deal with today, and today's tasks," he told a building wind he could feel on his face, and smell in the air.

Looking back on Sunday Night:

Mugs had gone back after that incident. A job's a job, and he had a reputation to uphold. But spying that man sitting on the bench next to her—he hadn't done anything. Couldn't chance it.

Something about the look of the man—like a guardian angel or something? *He remembered having to make room on his seat in grammar school so his guardian angel could sit next to him.* "Silly nuns," he whispered into the darkness of his room.

Monday morning, Mugs Nightshade was laying low at the Ludlow motel—reliving and wondering what to do about last night's cockup. He needed time to figure out his next move. In addition, and most importantly, he hadn't completed his latest job. Hadn't gotten close enough to the woman. His employer needed good solid leverage. *On top of that...I almost got snagged myself when checking out the layout.* This job was definitely not coming off according to plan. *And having to go back. Disgusting.*

On the other side of the coin, Mugs felt extremely lucky he had survived—period. Fights, even gunplay weren't strangers to him—but trying to escape by suddenly careening down a dirt road in pitch-blackness—a road potted with holes and rocks at sixty miles per hour, and with nothing but parking lights to show the road...all them bushes-looking things on both sides of the road...two sharp curves right off in maybe a five-hundred foot distance...rabbits caught in his running lights scurrying across the road from both sides. Mugs shook his head hard—as if he could physically just make last night go away. Disappear forever. A city man, he had been very scared indeed on that desert road in the dark.

Then driving back out to that castle-looking house completely in the dark. *Okay,* on the main road at least, but no streetlights, no turn-off sign. The white lines faded.

Consequently, even though having survived last night, he was primarily not a happy man this morning. And not sure what to do next. Not a state Mugs liked—or often found himself in.

He walked over to his room's window, pulled the curtain back a bit, then hazarded a look outside. At breakfast, the Ludlow Café waiter told him there was a Dairy Queen in town. One of his favorites—in Chicago, and on the road. Even though he'd just eaten, Mugs contemplated going to get a shake. Once he figured out his next move and checked out, the chocolate shake would be his reward.

Not, that he was hungry or complaining about the food at the Ludlow Café. Pancakes, eggs, bacon—all top-notch. In line with his thoughts, Mugs unconsciously rubbed his stomach like a cartoon or vaudeville character. *Good food at that place.* He planned, though, to never eat there again. "No way will I ever return to this damn desert," he said aloud—his iconic Route 66 motel room the only witness to his resolve.

Further on the room front, Mugs was surprised and pleased to find the place after his failures in the desert darkness of last night. It was a nice clean room—with a mini-refrigerator no less. *And the café right next door.* When he pulled in last night, Mugs was still rattled indeed, but in retrospect this morning, he felt not only pretty darned lucky to have survived, but also to find a nice vacant motel room.

However, "What do I do now?" He pulled the curtain back a bit more so he could see out into the nearly empty motel parking area. *Only two cars.* Neither were red. "He doesn't know I'm here." Still, his exit plan via John Wayne airport was too risky now, with a crazed vigilante-cop on the loose hunting him down.

Though it wasn't a cop car gunning for him, at one point getting within feet of his bumper—looked more like a pickup. Red for sure. But Mug's experienced "gut" told him it was the same guy eyeing him in Penny's. *Or,* he deviously thought—and again from experience and instinct—somebody playing at being a cop? A vigilante? But how would an ordinary person have a clue about him? Or who he was?

Mugs shook his head again, not as hard, and this time from dissatisfaction that he couldn't figure out for sure what was going on. *Had to be that cop.*

"I need to get back home. Somehow." Mugs left the window, went over to his still partly straight bed and sat down, then he let his torso fall back onto the part of the bed's surface he hadn't rumpled last night.

Sure, he knew his client would be unhappy—but hopefully not really bent out of shape enough to put a hit out on him. This politician and his daughter weren't anything to her—just leverage items. *I'm not in danger of getting whacked myself.* But not getting close enough to his target and getting something to take back his client could use for influence to get her way? *Not good.*

It was the crazy vigilante guy out there he was more afraid of. And right now, he needed to think some more.

The crazy maniac chasing me at seventy or eighty on that narrow two lane main highway, then having to evade him by swerving off when he saw a cutout after a curve. Speeding as best he could down that god-awful dirt road. Then those horrible moments sitting in pitch-blackness with no idea where he was, waiting until he was sure the maniac had passed and wasn't coming back looking for him.

It was a miracle I had the balls to go back out there. He knew that dirt road escape had traumatized him in ways Mugs was yet to figure out.

Even now, looking at the ceiling while lying back on the bed, Mugs managed to shudder. Last night he had barely been able to turn around, the dirt road was so narrow, rutted, and high banked. When he finally did get back going in the right direction, he still didn't turn on his big headlights—just parking ones. *Too risky.*

He came to the Mojave as a hunter, he would be leaving as the hunted.

Mugs sat up—and though prefaced with a sigh—he said with renewed resolve and confidence, "I need to think about how to get out of here alive this morning." *Not relive how I got here...indeed, that was last night.* And Mugs Nightshade knew he needed to deal with today, and today's task. Getting out of this damn desert without being whacked himself. He planned to make it back to Paulina Street alive.

Chapter Eight
Endgames For Real

From LC's journal: *Wish I'd kept friends with my Cooper relatives after starting again here. Wonder who was actually the real winner in that game of Gypsy pride squabbling stuff in Chicago, and then claiming my opals were theirs? Viola says only time will tell. Maybe there was something I should have done differently…*

Tuesday Morning:

Captain Austin had lied to him. Monday was not his last day on I-40 Caltrans duty. Back again on the duty roster. This morning, however, Officer Ben Bellaeu was again pleased— *maybe.* Perfect situation to keep his eye out, *or* face up to the truth. It was the usual moderate level of traffic, mainly seasoned good-driving truckers—and the presence of his black and white alone slowed the other hotheads down. *Even the red car drivers,* he mused with irony—as he often did at his own biased foible about red cars.

With deliberation, he puffed-up his substantial cheeks and blew out a walloping lung full of air. His gut was telling him the Fixer was still right under his nose. But for once, Ben wasn't sure if his instincts were on the right track. *Maybe just foolishness on my gut's part?* For *if* the Fixer was as smart as Ben now surmised he was, the SOB should be long gone. Headed back to his little hidey-hole—somewhere back east—like Chicago, was his guess. *How?* That was the part he hadn't yet figured out.

For the moment, he could just sit in his cruiser and watch. One of the Caltrans workers on site even promised to bring him back a Subway sandwich and drink from Newberry Springs for lunch, and the porta-potty wasn't that far from his cruiser. *Perfect* for what he needed—time alone. Time to keep a look out, assess his situation, and then lay out plans for his next move. *If there was one.* His seat was back as far as it would go, his legs stretched out comfortably, and his window closed tight against marauding dust-devils. Wouldn't want dust all over his freshly pressed pants legs. *Seems to happen every time.*

He knew that immediately after Noiseless, the dead hit man in the culvert had been identified, all area law enforcement had started watching the airports—Orange County, LA, Burbank, Vegas. A Fixer alert warning had even gone out—that he was probably heading to California to ensure the job got done this time. He was a hit man with a reputation for being an insurance policy.

And plain logic said the thug had to fly in and out from somewhere. Ben initially thought, *my last chance for a confrontation could be at an airport.* If he got the right airport. Ben's gut-guess was John Wayne—though he wasn't sure why.

However, after sitting and thinking throughout the entire morning, then through lunch, Ben Bellaeu eventually reached an inevitable conclusion—their game was over. And he blamed himself. *Screwed up on that one curve.*

Indeed, after all his pondering, Ben's emotions and thoughts ended up laced in retrospective regret and self admonishment—*knowing I should have side slammed that car before the curve.* Instead, caution for a possible approaching car had caused him to back off—just for a moment. *Then the Fixer was gone.* His only excuse for such stupidity? Darkness and caution. *So much for my "electrifying mystique" about darkness.*

The Fixer is going to escape. If he hasn't already. Two mornings now of regret. Ben further cursed his actions on Sunday night aloud. "What the hell kind of caretaker am I?" He looked outside. "A damn terrible one."

A Mojave wind funnel from nowhere snuck onto the median strip—causing sand to start swirling all around, even forcing the Caltrans workers to seek shelter in their trucks and cars. Ben slipped his hand into his pocket and fingered his lucky medal with *Facit Justitia* engraved on it. *Even the gods are scolding me.*

"But I can't win them all, can I?" he responded to anthropomorphized Mojave wind and dust-driven accusations. "I really did try." Indeed, he'd spent all of Monday searching from the Penny's area, past Shiné, even lunched at Ludlow café, then headed east for a bit toward Needles.

"You didn't try hard enough," the wind protested as it blasted his door with gusto.

The growing and judgmental dustbowl suddenly began to swirl and pound the entire worksite. "But I can't help it's a draw this time. Can I?"

"More like a stalemate," the Mojave winds insisted on the last words.

Mugs stretched his legs out even farther in the spacious backseat area. He was very proud of himself—they were already into Arizona.

Yesterday in his Ludlow Motel room, *Monday it was,* what to do came to Mugs out of the blue while he was half thinking about Dairy Queen and trying to remember when checkout time was.

"Perfect," he informed his motel room as soon as his escape plan jelled into its final form. Mugs immediately called his rental car company at the airport and made the necessary arrangements. Consequently, Monday night, Mugs Nightshade had an excellent night's sleep for the first time since he'd arrived in this *damned desert.*

At barely dawn Tuesday morning, a chauffeur driven limousine and a Hertz employee riding out with him, arrived at his hotel. The Hertz employee took Mug's rental car back—and after he settled up for his room, the chauffeur whisked Mugs, a bag of Route 66 items purchased at the cafe, and his one roller bag into a sleek jet-black, tinted-window-glass limousine. Then they headed eastward bound. Chicago their destination.

No driving back to the LA area or Las Vegas for Mugs, just heading directly east. *Seeing Route 66 in a limo. What an idea.* It was going to cost him a fortune, but the whole scenario made him smile. *Who would expect somebody to do a thing like that?* Only he, Mugs Nightshade, would come up with such a brilliant solution.

And to top it all off, his client called Mugs on his cell phone around Kingman, Arizona. His "hit" was successful. Moore had been intimidated and caved. Just Mugs's presence in The Mojave had been enough. *No need* to send a message through menacing acts. It did concern Mugs how law enforcement and Winston knew he was in California? He guessed, *that damn cop in that damn desert.* Still, damn cop or not, the knowledge he wasn't as stealthy as he thought, was for sure disturbing.

"I'll be calling on your caretaking expertise again down the road. Count on it," his client had assured him. The word caretaker sounded a little better the way she said it this time. Not like a janitor, but like someone who takes care of things. A more uptown way of saying "Fixer."

Extraordinary as it was though, out of that conversation, Mugs Nightshade considered for the first time *not* taking care of anyone's problems. *Ever again.* He'd never before given quitting a thought—but now, *there the idea was.* One day he just might get caught?

Introspectively—also a change for Mugs—he looked hard at himself in the mirror next to the glass see-through window in back of the limousine—and thought about how his barber in Chicago was maintaining his black hair. By the time his chauffeur, Harold, next pulled into a station for gas—Mugs had made the monumental decision to let his hair go grey.

After they'd both used the bathroom and Mugs was comfortably ensconced in the plush luxury of his limousine's interior, he was again startled by where his thoughts took him.

I just want to grow nightshade on a fence somewhere. Somewhere no one else knew where he was. *Yes,* and starting off by not having his hair dyed anymore fit right into his new Mugs Nightshade vision.

With his mind racing, Mugs thought of the perfect spot. *Yes,* he would find a modest rambler in one of the Northwest suburbs. Maybe around the airport, or Niles, or Avondale? Who would guess The Fixer was in their neighborhood? *Tending my nightshade.*

While standing next to him in the bathroom, his chauffeur Harold had mentioned a chauffeur friend, Malcolm, in Springfield, Illinois that he hoped to see on his way back. Funny thing, Harold further expanded on his good fortune of landing a drive to Chicago—Malcolm had just driven his employer and daughter from Southern Illinois to California—then the father back to Illinois. "Funny world, now ain't it?" Mugs took Harold's revelation as a big time omen—yet another uncharacteristic occurrence for him.

Then and there, Mugs resolved, quite firmly—there certainly would not be a next time.

For sure, it was time for Mugs Nightshade to start growing his own nightshade along his own fence. He'd lucked out this time *with a draw.* Or was it a stalemate? He never could keep all that snooty chess talk straight.

Chapter Nine
Future Game Matches

From LC's journal: Viola says I'm loco planting all those trees in a circle like around the driveway road. But I keep telling her, every castle got to have its big-time entrance. Otherwise, all you got is a big house. Besides, I'm a planning on seeing my grandkids married in there. By then the whole thing will be real nice like. Yep, right out here in the desert. I can just see it now.

Wedding Sunday Morning..

Once again, after first giving the library a try, Leiv ended up spending his pre-dawn hours in LC 's copula. First anticipating, then savoring the sunrise. Days were already getting shorter as fall progressed and winter threatened. But these burst-of-color sunrises, no matter the time, still managed to capture him with their beauty.

As Leiv looked around his Shiné world in the infancy moments of sunrise—with a ray of light struggling to shine in through his eastern-most window—he thought he might actually be happy. And he wasn't sure why—in that Melissa was still gone, never to be touched or kissed or talked to again. *How can I possible be happy?* But for the first time since she died, that fateful night's drive on the Congress didn't immediately invade upon his mind's eye, or dampen his emotions and heart with the very thought of her.

Emotionally caught off guard, he further savored the sunrise without other intruding thoughts for several moments.

When he returned to pondering current events, Leiv was disappointed in that there was still no resolution on Lucca's fire from the Fire Marshall. Nonetheless, in a back recess of his mind, he believed Tim Teague had attempted to burn Lucca out, figuring Tim wanted the land for his latest nudist colony expansion. As the teenage Caretaker had so aptly pointed out, *"It costs money to get naked."* Unfortunately Leiv had no proof—just his gut nagging at him. If Tim *had* done it, he'd get away with it. At least Lucca had survived.

But even with the fire resolution disappointment, Leiv's feeling of happiness remained. Confusing him a tad, in that all was not settled in his mind on other fronts, either. The Needles Sheriff's Department had informed Glover the hit on Adeleine was off? *But they can't be certain, can they?* Indeed, how would they *know* for sure? Glover had mumbled something about Winston Moore saying everything was alright now—no one threatening Adeleine anymore. For sure, Leiv was immensely relieved. Indeed, Winston had also called his daughter Adeleine last night.

Nonetheless, his instincts didn't trust Winston. Maybe he even instigated the whole event to claim victimhood of a type— leading to some kind of "win" he wanted? A solution which very much fit the man he had known. Devious. With winning always his ultimate goal. But whatever was going on with Winston and his cohorts—if there were cohorts—they would get away with whatever it was.

Then, from wherever inexplicable realizations come from—Leiv also saw clearly, and addressing a completely different aspect of his life—that as a teenager, and then on throughout his whole life, he had always preferred living in what he thought of as "the world." New York, Chicago, London,

Paris.... But now, at whatever lifespan age he called himself —
Leiv knew and felt he loved LC's Shiné. It was home.

He was stunned. "Has Winston somehow done that for
me?" The connection was not obvious. Maybe one day he'd
figure it out.

But there was not time enough for Leiv to digest his
realizations. Take it all in. Much less turn his new truths around
in his mind.

No, time was short. He and Adeleine had a wedding to
"put on" — and he would start their day by making Adeleine
breakfast. *Not that easy to drop my caretaker role,* even though
Winston's call said all danger was gone. His daughter could come
home whenever she wanted.

Leiv wasn't sure he wanted her to leave....

"Which plan are you going to propose?" Leiv asked
Margaret. Even with everything else going on, the future of Shiné
was still a worry nagging at him.

She feigned ignorance, and said through a sly smile,
"What plans are you talking about?"

Margaret was actually sitting at a two-table configuration
several rows behind him with Elizabeth-May Logan, Hermit
Chan, Mary Jones, Doc Will Walker, Walker Johns, & Adeleine.
However, she had temporarily come up to his "honored" front
table near the marriage platform to sit and talk for a few
moments with him and her son Glover.

Glover played along with his mother, adding his own
two-cents tease in the process. "He wants to know how soon he
can strip and go cavorting around Tim's desert playground."

Leiv made an appropriate face.

Margaret's tone turned serious, "I know you have to sign
off on any land project. And you want to know what you'll be
facing down the road?"

Leiv nodded.

She reached over and put her hand atop of his resting on the table. Her hands were warm, comforting. *I'm a lucky man,* Leiv thought. *Having my father's first love close.*

In line with Leiv's thoughts, Margaret said, "Your father told me once way back when, that just because somebody else is playing a game, doesn't mean you have to participate. That is, if you can get out of it."

"You mentioned that to me Sunday—"

Glover interrupted with a chuckling sound.

"I know, and Glover's heard me say it a million times." Then—to Glover's obvious chagrin—she blew her son a kiss off the palm of her hand.

"But when there's power and authority you can't escape...." Leiv suggested.

"You're stuck," she agreed.

Leiv had dealt with the reality of power and authority all his working life—politicians, bureaucrats, DA's, police chiefs, mobsters, gangs. Memories he didn't want to revisit this wedding morning. Quickly, he forced his mind back into the direction of Shiné's possible future.

Margaret continued, "But at this stage of the game, I still have a move." She smiled mischievously.

"Not a 'stalemate,' as they say in chess?" Leiv asked. Margaret was up to something—which pleased him very much indeed.

"More like a time-out." She smiled at him for a very long moment, pressing his hand tighter with what Leiv took as an expression of fondness. "If I don't get my responses in by the deadline. Tomorrow. So soon...." She spread her hands for a few seconds in a gesture of helplessness. "What with all the excitement going on in Shiné and my getting older and forgetful...or...or...." She smiled.

He turned his hand over, smiled back at her, and fought a lump rising in his throat while reciprocating her renewed hand-embrace.

Without further ado, she got up and returned to her table with her friends—old and new. Leiv was also pleased to see Adeleine fitting in with his family, and "family of friends" quite nicely.

As he watched Margaret walk the short distance between tables, her long and flowing tie-dyed-looking skirt imbued her with a floating-like look. *Old and forgetful, my foot,* Leiv appraised with grateful humor.

Relieved on that front, knowing Margaret had a plan in the works, Leiv returned his attention to Hester's wedding.

The sunrise had been grand, heralding in a beautiful morning for the small gathering to enjoy the weather and proceedings outside in LC's circular expanse in front of Rhodes Castle. No wind. No blowing sand. Temperature around seventy-five degrees. And this special morning's grand deep-red sunrise also left a faint glow—a halo-like effect to the sky underneath which Hester Miller and David Milhouse would exchange wedding vows. *Other-worldly almost.*

After Margaret's departure, and after a few moments of silence in which Leiv and Glover each got lost in their own thoughts—live wedding-style music began softly playing in the background. Leiv actually knew it was a list put together by Marilyn LeBue, David's friend, music expert, and co-film collaborator.

Providing the music were amateur violinist, Brad Temper and cohort-musicians in a Needles based group—volunteers who all loved playing at events just like this. They were gathered in front as a string quartet to the left of the area Pastor Apply and the bride and groom would assemble.

After listening for a bit, Leiv thought they were doing an excellent job—which pleased him. He very much wanted

Hester's big day to go well. Being at "his place" he felt a responsibility everything went off according to plan.

Leiv glanced down at his program on the table in front of him. It was printed on dusty-rose colored paper with dark purple printing, and he found Marilyn's music list footnoted in small print near the bottom—"A Midsummer Night's Dream," "Wedding March," "Lakmé: El Dúo de la Flor," "Salut d'Amour," "Arios," and "Für Elise." All "Transcribed for Strings," the footnote further explained.

Not a classical music buff himself, Leiv didn't recognize any of the names, but he was sure his deceased wife Melissa would have. Indeed, she had personally selected the music for their wedding. Again, Leiv's mind and emotions didn't go down their usual painful-memory path. Instead, he whimsically wondered if they would play the traditional "Here Comes the Bride" when Hester and David finally appeared. *Maybe that was the "Wedding March" on the program?*

Leiv took another moment to look around a bit. One couldn't avoid they were outside in the Mojave Desert—but the unique majesty of Rhodes Castle itself, and his and Adeleine's hard work had transformed LCs front courtyard into—well he wasn't sure what they'd made it like—but thought it quite nice. Hopefully Hester and David would, too.

Charlie White and Pete Lily were sitting at the table across the bridal aisle from he and Glover—an aisle for Hester and David to walk down which he had personally laid out from a roll of red felt-like stuff. Both the movie-maker and photographer were fidgeting with their hands, and generally looking quite nervous. *Almost as if they were the ones getting hitched.*

Leiv didn't believe there was going to be a flower girl, or ring-boy, or father of the bride. None of that conforming traditional stuff. No best man and bridesmaid stuff. Not for Hester, he didn't think. Still, he looked around quickly to confirm his suspicion. He was sure it would just be David and Hester walking together up to the pastor and saying their vows. *Simple.*

He also glanced Margaret's way and saw she looked comfortable and happy. So did Adeleine. He also noticed this time, Douglas "Hermit" Chan was sitting next to Elizabeth-May. *Hmmm.* That situation also pleased him, and unconsciously a smile spread across his face. *More romance?*

Abruptly—if String Quartets can be abrupt—Brad's little group started playing, "Here's Comes the Bride."

Leiv turned in his seat—and there they were. Hester and David, arm in arm, walking solemnly down their "red-carpet," heading toward anticipated happiness.

"Was your wedding big?" Glover, having turned around also, asked softly.

"Not really." Leiv remembered the service and reception well. The ceremony had been small, even though held in Melissa's large, dark, and rather cavernous parish church with its arching dome-like ceiling—the actual service was at a more intimate side-altar for the "Virgin Mary." *I can still see it.* The ceremony was officiated by a priest whose name Leiv could no longer remember, though he could still visualize his rather pleasant looking, but serious-in-demeanor oval face.

Somehow, someway, the couple Hester Miller and David Milhouse looked perfect as they proceeded to the area between the two front tables. Pastor Apply had an open book in his hand, and a large smile spread across his face.

David wore finely creased "dress-jeans"—Leiv guessed Hester had done the pressing—a blue chambray shirt, a silly looking dark blue red-stripped bowtie, and a dark blue sports jacket that looked sixties-era. Oddly, his wedding-attire choices seemed to capture his film-making and set designer worldliness, and his newly acquired *bon vivant* Mojave Desert off-the-grid role.

Hester, to Leiv's eye had chosen and dressed true to her nature, perceived identity, and penchant for the outlandish. He thought her this morning, the prettiest he'd ever seen. Her dress was floral patterned in blue and dark purple with a lilac sash tied in a bow; her headdress was red with a thin mauve veil. He couldn't see her shoes, but in her right arm she carried a dozen white roses.

Marvelous, Leiv wanted to say, but didn't. *No need,* he thought. She could probably read his thoughts if so inclined. And for sure, she was most probably thinking about more important things than the impression she might be making on him.

Leiv smiled inwardly at the thought of his new neighbors Hester and David. Indeed, he was sure LC and Everett would also have liked them as Shiné property owners. His present to the couple was wrapped up in paper, stuffed in her gypsy-tea can, with a bow on top. It was the deed to their land. Free and clear.

When the couple stopped in front of Pastor Apply, ready to take their vows—Glover leaned in close to Leiv and said barely above a whisper, "Don't be surprised by what you hear, Leiv. It's pretty short, but to the point."

Leiv had no idea what Glover was talking about, but he made sure he listened more carefully than he might have otherwise. Hester and David spoke in unison, a memorized and obviously rehearsed statement of their commitment.

"…and we vow to be *caretakers* for each other of our love, our aspirations, our dreams, and our lives."

What a schmaltz I am, Leiv found himself thinking with disdain, while simultaneously needing to force back a moistness that wanted to invade his eyes.

Epilogue

Several weeks later:

Lloyd slipped away to use Rhodes Castle's hall restroom.

"You know," Leiv said, seizing the moment, and without segue from explaining to Glover and their friend Lloyd how port wine was made. "I think I know who 'the caretaker' is."

"Lots of caretakers in the world, Leiv. Which one are you talking about?"

Not rising to Glover's question, Leiv waited. He figured Shiné's Police Chief knew *whom* he was talking about. Also, Leiv was so relaxed after several *aperitifs* of Sonderman's Port this time, he didn't feel up to sparing.

It was Saturday night again in LC's withdrawing room, and his regular guests had already snacked for a while on some excellent mini-quiches Adeleine made—then washed them down with wine, or *aperitifs* like he had.

After a moment, Glover eventually added, "I'm guessing you mean our vigilante 'Caretaker?' At least that's what they're calling him in the various Sheriff's Department locker rooms."

"Yep." Though Leiv didn't think the moniker exactly fitting—especially if you were a criminal on the receiving end. He took a quick look Margaret's way, sitting in her regular spot on the loveseat to his left. She was talking to Adeleine next to her—hopefully unawares of her son and his conversation. "Officer—"

Glover cut him off quite abruptly, "Don't say his name."

"Like with Macbeth?"

Glover tsked out the corner of his mouth. "Of course not. There's no curse I know of associated with his name or actions. And," he added, "we aren't actors."

"To misquote, we're '...just poor players, strutting and fretting our hour upon the stage...'"

This time Glover moaned with exaggerated emphasis, then accentuated his dramatic response with a follow on. "Spare me, please." Then he tsked one more time, even louder, before adding in a theatrical mocking voice, "And that particular passage actually goes, 'Out, out, brief candle! Life's but a walking shadow, a poor player that struts and frets his hour upon the stage and then is heard no more: it is a tale told by an idiot, full of sound and fury, signifying nothing.'"

"Are you sure?" Leiv was astounded at Glover's quoting from Macbeth, but wasn't sure why he was so surprised. *Just not a fit for the "John Wayne" image I like cloaking Glover in?*

"Nope, I'm not sure. Shooting from the hip."

That was more like the Glover he knew, but Leiv remained silent. *More to my brother than I know.*

Indeed, they both fell into companionable quiet for a few moments. When returning to Ben Bellaeu, the name that must not be said, Leiv said, "Should we do something? Say something?"

Another moment passed before Glover said, "Or not."

Intangible as it was, and for reasons Leiv couldn't explain if pressed, Leiv knew both of them were in agreement—and without looking at each other, or communicating with each other in a straightforward manner. Ben Bellaeu had taken out the Noiseless Killer. But there was no proof, and neither of them were about to continue digging. Though Leiv heard a *"for now,"* unsaid in Glover's tone. But he left it by agreeing, "Or not."

Glover changed the topic "You know the county meeting was Friday?"

"Forgot." He looked over at Margaret and thought he should have asked her about the deadline. His stomach immediately churned as he thought about Shiné's future. *Oh no.*

"Well, on the way down to San Bernardino, her car failed and she had to pull over on the side of the road. Fortunately, before going down through the pass." He shook his head. "Anyway, she called road service and they came and got her started."

"Did she call you?"

"Oh yeah, I kept her on the phone all the time. A woman by herself."

Once again both men instinctively knew why her late model Lexus had failed. *On purpose.*

Glover added, "Unfortunately she missed the county meeting. Didn't get any Shiné input into the selection-hat."

Dear Margaret. A reprieve for Shiné being forced to enter the current world. Maybe only temporary—but a timeout for sure.

Then after several more moments of companionable silence, Glover said, "Deputy Brad claims that statistically, Shiné is a hot bed of crime. Or a mischievous-hot-spot to put Deputy Tanya's spin on it." Glover quickly held up his hands towards Leiv in a stopping gesture, then leaned back against his rocker back. Glover then answered his disbelieving look, "It's *their* naming convention—not mine."

"First names only? They sound like cartoon—"

Glover covered his mouth with his hand. "Don't go there, Leiv. This isn't the time for me to start laughing."

"You're not in uniform. You can be as foolish as me."

Glover lowered his hand, but tightened his lips in a holding-it-in manner. But his eyes clearly reflected his internal merriment.

Nevertheless, Leiv couldn't immediately stop himself. "I can see the cartoon intro now—"

"I asked you not to—"

"Deputy Dan and Deputy Tanya, super-powered deputies off to save the world." Leiv did manage to keep his hands affixed in his lap. "And they'd be wearing super-human type capes and big "D"s on their chests...."

"You've had too much Harvey's."

Leiv shook his head. "Port actually. And so have you."

* * * * *

Judge Rhodes had invited him to his Saturday night shindig up at the castle a couple days ago, but he'd begged off. Wasn't yet up to so much people stuff. *No,* he needed a few more weeks to regain his composure when it came to being around other folks and having to tell his story.

Besides, Jasmine was spending much more time with him now, even in the evenings, and even though he was camped out in a tiny trailer. She'd offered for him to stay with her and Tim until he got set up again—but no way was he going to spend any more time around that man of hers than he had to.

Fortunately, he could see their marriage souring with each passing day. Suspicion *is hard to deal with.* He smiled.

Now this Monday morning, Lucien "Lucca" Fabero wasn't quite sure what he felt about the "things" being offloaded in front of him from the two trailer-beds pulled up where his old doublewide had sat for many a year.

The shell of his double wide was completely gone, the property cleaned up of fire-scorched remnants, rough ground was filled and graded where needed, and even some new trees had been planted. Oleander and some kind of Christmas-tree shaped firs. Even a line of palms near the road. Most miraculously for him, his existing little orchard garden—though showing some damage for sure—was still intact. Even the Fire Chief was surprised how his little trees made it through the inferno that had consumed his house. *Chief didn't know about the wind protected pocket he'd planted them in.*

Leiv was rebuilding his home for him with what Lucca thought Leiv called modules. Supposedly—somehow, someway, the futuristic looking cubes would be put together and still fall under the mobile home building permit he already had. The truck drivers were offloading these "things" as he watched. Supposedly there was a fancy kitchen, three types of heat, electric, pellet, and wood-burning already either built in, or set up for. And they already had strict instructions not to damage his fruit trees. It was like the Judge knew how important they were to him. *A Rhodes through and through, he is.*

Jasmine will love the new place, maybe stop worrying about me. She'd made friends with that new Adeleine lady up at the castle. *Good for her mental health.* Indeed, Lucca felt pretty good all-in-all, though there were still some lingering effects from the fire. His chest still hurt if he coughed too heavily, or laughed too loud. So all this new home stuff being done for him was a godsend.

That I don't deserve.

He walked a little closer, trying to be mindful of not getting in the way—but wanting to see as much as he could. It was a quiet morning, with a pale blue sky above—the aftermath of a rather ordinary sunrise. And for once, the Mojave winds were silent.

Carefully, he took in a deep breath, then slowly let it out as a sigh. What was done, was done. *Still,* burning up my home— a home Everett Rhodes had so graciously set up for him to live in, was not something he would "accidently" let happen.

But he had, hadn't he? Spreading gasoline and then stumbling? After all, he was an old man now. And he had to get Tim Teague out, now didn't he? But carrying an open gasoline can, and stumbling when there was nothing to stumble over. And the firefighters that could have gotten hurt. Some friends even. *Had I actually wanted this to happen?* Well not to burn up my home actually, but to get Tim out of Jasmine's life?

Indeed, Lucca had tried not to pry into Jasmine's life over the last couple weeks. But he was pretty darned sure—along with everyone else in town and down below where Jasmine and Tim lived—that she was divorcing the bum at last. Everybody figured he tried to burn up her father's home to get the land cheap so he could further his money making.

Accident, or on purpose—*who could ask for a better outcome?*

Now, standing by his little trees he'd taken particular care weren't in harm's way, savoring he was still alive, and happy Jasmine was going to divorce Tim—Lucca's smile broadened.

And just this morning, hadn't he heard Leiv quite proudly introduce him to the truck driver bringing in the pieces of his new home as—"The Caretaker?"

The Caretakers
Named Characters by Novel of First Appearance

Lucien "Lucca" Fabero	Rhodes	The Caretakers
CHP Officer Benjamin Bellaeu	Rhodes	The Caretakers
Mugs Nightshade	Rhodes	The Movie-Maker
Mary Jones	Rhodes	The Mojave-Stone
Adeleine Moore	Rhodes	The Caretakers
Winston Moore	Rhodes	The Caretakers
Malcolm	Rhodes	The Caretakers
Walker Johns	Rhodes	The Mojave-Stone
Mark	Rhodes	The Caretakers
Fire Chief Parnell	Rhodes	The Caretakers
Leigh-Everett "Leiv" Rhodes	Rhodes	The Mojave-Stone
Glover "Dusty" Deers	Rhodes	The Mojave-Stone
Margaret Deers	Rhodes	The Mojave-Stone
Chef Jack	Rhodes	The Mojave-Stone
Charlie White	Rhodes	The Movie-Maker
David Milhouse	Rhodes	The Movie-Maker
Hester Miller - "HM"	Rhodes	The Mojave-Stone
Pete "PL" Lily	Rhodes	The Movie-Maker
Jasmine Fabero Teague	Rhodes	The Caretakers
Dr. William "Will" Walker.	Rhodes	The Mojave-Stone
Elizabeth-May Logan	Rhodes	The Movie-Maker
Douglas "Hermit" Chan	Rhodes	The Movie-Maker
Pastor Lloyd Apply	Rhodes	The Mojave-Stone
Becca	Rhodes	The Caretakers
Dobie	Rhodes	The Mojave-Stone
Nadya Rhodes Collins	Rhodes	The Mojave-Stone
Sydney Collins	Rhodes	The Mojave-Stone
Deputy Sheriff Brad Temper	Rhodes	The Mojave-Stone
Deputy Sheriff Tanya Lewis	Rhodes	The Movie-Maker
Marilyn LeBue	Rhodes	The Movie-Maker
Timothy "Tim" Teague	Rhodes	The Caretakers
Nathan "Nate" Johnson	Rhodes	The Caretakers
Keith Meldon	Rhodes	The Caretakers
Adele Mason	Rhodes	The Caretakers
Terry Hall	Rhodes	The Caretakers

ACKNOWLEDGEMENTS

As always, my gratitude goes to my excellent editors—Mike Foley and Kitty Kladstrup. This story would not be published without them.

To my relatives, friends, fellow authors, and readers—thanks for your continuing words of encouragement. I can never properly say how much your support means to me.

I'm also most grateful to my Route 66 and Public Safety Writers Association (PSWA) friends and business owners who always so graciously provide information on animals, politics, law-enforcement, Route 66, and local lore. And to Robert "Bob" Haig, author of *Fire Horses*, a retired Detroit Firefighter, for sharing his experiences.

And to my dear editor for so long, Virginia Moody, whose "angel spirit" now continues with me in my heart—thank you for being my friend.

Madeline (M.M.) Gornell's mystery novels include— PSWA award winners *Uncle Si's Secret* and *Lies of Convenience* (also a Hollywood Book Festival Honorable Mention), *Death of a Perfect Man*, and *Reticence of Ravens* (a finalist for the Eric Hoffer 2011 fiction Prize, the da Vinci Eye for cover art, and the Montaigne Medal for most thought-provoking book). *Counsel of Ravens* (a London Book Festival Honorary Mention and LA Book Festival Runner-Up) is her first sequel, and was a continuation of Hubert Champion's Mojave saga. Rhodes—The Caretakers is the third novel in her series featuring Leiv Rhodes's Mojave saga that began in Rhodes—The Mojave-Stone.

She continues to be inspired by historic Route 66, and this, her third Rhodes novel, reflects that continuing fascination. Madeline lives with her husband and assorted canines in the Mojave High Desert near the internationally revered Route 66.

From LC's journal, on page one-hundred-and-two, where Leigh Cooper Rhodes explains the origin of his town's name—Shiné.

Viola likes to show our boys the stones in morning light. Sitting as they do up top of the house, mornings usually, letting the sun make them glitter, sparkle, shine. André calls it shiny, and it comes out his little mouth as shy-knee. Viola's got a soft spot for that one, and has started saying the name of our place shy-knee like the boy. She may have made shy-knee a reality, but it's little André who really named the place.
Thinking I'm gonna be changing the spelling too, and with one of them little marks at the end. Make it fancy, befitting a Leigh Cooper Rhodes kind of town.

Then he'd printed, in block letter across a whole page:

SHINÉ

www.ingramcontent.com/pod-product-compliance
Lightning Source LLC
Chambersburg PA
CBHW031426200626
46814CB00016B/2493